OUTSIDERS

Paul E. Kelly

PublishAmerica
Baltimore

© 2006 by Paul E. Kelly.
All rights reserved. No part of this book may be reproduced, stored in a retrieval system or transmitted in any form or by any means without the prior written permission of the publishers, except by a reviewer who may quote brief passages in a review to be printed in a newspaper, magazine or journal.

First printing

All characters appearing in this work are fictitious. Any resemblance to real persons, living or dead, is purely coincidental.

At the specific preference of the author, PublishAmerica allowed this work to remain exactly as the author intended, verbatim, without editorial input.

ISBN: 1-4241-2076-4
PUBLISHED BY PUBLISHAMERICA, LLLP
www.publishamerica.com
Baltimore

Printed in the United States of America

OUTSIDERS

CHAPTER ONE

From the hillside overlooking the prairie, Red Eagle watched the long column of white canvas, powdered with dust, wending its way westward. Explosions of dust engulfed spokes as wagon wheels broke through sun-baked crust. Mules pulled a few wagons, but most were hitched to oxen. Men walked along side the oxen, leading them. Those with mules sat on the front of the wagon box, slouched forward, reins in hands, hats pulled down hard on their heads shielding their faces from the sun. Others rode horseback while some, mostly women, walked along side as if shepherding the column, making sure it kept to the worn path. Children played tag with the wagons, lagging behind, then running to catch up.

Red Eagle watched these strange outsiders as they passed through on their way to some faraway place. He had watched them before and feared one day that faraway place would fill up and these intruders would become like the rising backwaters of a beaver dam. He stood motionless, gazing at the wagons until they vanished in a hazy layer of dust. The late afternoon sunshine illuminated the cloud, giving it an orange glow. When the dust cloud disappeared, so had the wagons. He wondered where these people came from, but most of all he longed to know where they were going, where the faraway place was. He would speak with the old one, Gray Cloud.

Early next morning, Red Eagle sat outside Gray Cloud's tepee, waiting for the old warrior to emerge. The tepee was next to the biggest tree in camp. The tree was old and wind-crippled, but its size showed the respect accorded Gray Cloud. He was a Chief Elder who as a young warrior had proved his bravery in many battles.

Hanging from a leather thong stretched between two of the tree limbs was a beaded headband, a necklace of colored stones and a loin apron of hide, but what caught Red Eagle's eye was the hunting knife. It was the envy of the village. His people had few metal objects and the knife was a highly prized possession. Years ago Gray Cloud had taken it from a fur hunter.

Red Eagle stared at the tree. In many ways, it was like Gray Cloud, old and gnarled, wearing the scars of its struggle with the elements, yet standing proud and defiant. The sun was two hours old when Red Eagle heard Gray Cloud stirring inside the tepee, followed by the chanting of his morning prayers. When the chanting stopped, Red Eagle scrambled to his feet. Gray Cloud stepped outside.

"Good morning, Red Eagle. Why do you honor me with your presence?" Gray Cloud asked.

"Good morning Gray Cloud. I am bothered by something. Sleep never came to me last night."

Gray Cloud strolled over and stood under the tree. "You are ready to take a wife?" he asked.

"No," answered Red Eagle, "I am troubled about the strange outsiders who pass through our land on their way to a faraway place."

Gray Cloud walked over and stared at him closely. Red Eagle looked into the eyes of Gray Cloud. They were scarred, and the brown had turned a smoky color.

"You must chase all thoughts of these outsiders from your mind," said Gray Cloud.

"But tell me," pleaded Red Eagle, "where is this faraway place? And why do they go there?"

"They are the unwanted," said Gray Cloud, "and there is no faraway place."

"I don't understand," said Red Eagle. "Why are they unwanted? And if there is no faraway place, where are they going?"

"They have no destination. These strange ones have been banished from their tribe for some evil they have done and are destined to roam the earth forever."

Red Eagle pondered his words, then asked, "But, Gray Cloud, how do you know this to be true?"

Gray Cloud fell silent. He was not accustomed to having his wisdom challenged by tribal members, but he forgave Red Eagle because he was young and ignorant. "I know this to be the truth, because one does not leave his birth land unless he has some way wronged his people." Then turning his back to Red Eagle, he said, "We shall speak of this no more."

Red Eagle stood on the hillside, shading his eyes from the sun, searching for outsiders. All day he stayed there scanning the horizon but sighted nothing but the wind in the trees. He was sure there was a faraway place. Why else would these outsiders always travel with the rising sun at their backs? However, he would not dare mention this to Gray Cloud.

That day on the hillside, Red Eagle fashioned a plan that would change his life forever.

It was after dark when he returned home. "Where have you been?" his mother asked.

"I watch for the outsiders who pass through our land" he answered.

"Why do you waste the daylight?"

"I wish to know where is the faraway place they seek."

"You should have gone with your father on the hunt. It is not good that a young man spend so much time alone. When your father was your age, he was a father."

"I am not my father," said Red Eagle.

"No," she said, "you are a dreamer."

Red Eagle started to answer, but his mother picked up a water gourd and left the tepee.

Quickly going through his belongings, he dug out the water skin and the rawhide pouch his father had made for him. He put an extra pair of moccasins in the pouch, then rolled up a blanket and tied it tight with a strand of rawhide.

Looking outside to make sure no one was watching, he went to the back of the teepee and took strips of dried meat from the sun rack and stuffed the pouch full. With his belongings under his arm, he headed for the river. He would find that faraway place.

Red Eagle stopped and took a last look at the family tepee. He wanted to tell his mother goodby, but knew he couldn't. As he passed Gray Cloud's tepee, he remembered the hunting knife hanging from the leather thong. He crept to the tree, unhooked the knife, slipped it into his waistband, and ran for the river.

Holding the pouch and blanket above his head, he waded across the stream. When he reached the far bank, he filled the water skin. With the pouch and the skin slung across one shoulder and the blanket across the other, Red Eagle looked back across the river at his village. Reaching down, he fingered the hilt of. Gray Cloud's hunting knife and felt an ache in his heart, knowing he could never again return.

The night air was cool, and he felt strong. Running at a slow pace, he headed in the direction he had last seen the outsider's dust cloud. Throughout the night, Red Eagle kept up a steady pace; until he grew tired, then walked until he was rested.

Just before dawn he stopped and dug out some of the pimican, chewed on it and sipped water. Red Eagle shivered as a cold breeze swept over him like the icy breath of a wayward spirit. It was the coolest part of the day, that short span between daybreak and sunrise. Wrapped in a blanket, Red Eagle lay on his back and stared at the tiny fires in the sky that dared only come out when it was dark and would soon be chased away by the morning sun. When he was a little boy his father told him the tiny fires were holes in the sky. Red Eagle pulled the blanket tighter around him and slept. At mid-morning he was awakened by the brightness of the sun. He sat up and looked around, confused at his strange surroundings. A great feeling of loneliness swept over him as he realized he too was now an outsider.

CHAPTER TWO

Andy Moorehouse rode at the head of the column. This was his third trip as wagon master. Standing in his stirrups, he scanned the horizon. Then held his hand in the air, signaling the train to stop.

Frank Ortman rode up beside him. "Trouble, Moorehouse?" he asked.

"No, Mr. Ortman, we're just gonna take a short break, that's all." Moorehouse didn't like Ortman. He couldn't put his finger on it, but something about the man rubbed him the wrong way.

"You're not expecting hostile Indians, are you?"

"They ain't hostile, Mr. Ortman, just unpredictable."

"Well, if you think there's going to be trouble, I want to know."

"Look, Ortman, if or when I think there's gonna be any kinda trouble, I'll be sure to let you and everyone else know. Now, go on back to your wagon and let me do my job."

Ortman glared at Moorehouse, jerked his horse around and rode off.

Moorehouse figured about two and half more hours to Cobble Canyon. On his last trip through the canyon, a band of renegade Indians had surprised him. It had cost him two men. This time he wasn't taking any chances, and had sent his scout, David Daggett, on ahead to have a look. That had been noon the day before.

Moorehouse's two outriders, Luke Norton, and Jake Vines joined him. Emmett Jones, riding drag, held his position some three hundred yards behind the wagons.

"Dave should've been back by now," said Luke.

"We'll wait three hours," said Moorehouse. "If he ain't back by then, we'll camp here tonight. I want plenty of daylight left when we get to Cobble Canyon. Pass the word back to the train, and let Emmett know what's goin' on."

In the early afternoon on his second day of travel, Red Eagle spotted a distant dust cloud and stepped up his pace. He was tired and wished he had taken a pony. Once he had stolen Gray Cloud's hunting knife, he had become a thief, and in the eyes of his people, whether it was a stolen knife or a horse, made little difference. The punishment was the same: Banishment.

Inattentive in his thoughts, Red Eagle topped a rise and froze in place. Not more than fifty yards ahead of him, a man sat astride a sorrel pony facing the other way. And past him in the distance was the wagon train. Red Eagle dropped to his knees and crept backwards out of sight. Keeping low, he traversed the hillside to a clump of bushes from where he had a view of the entire wagon train. Wagons were strung out as far as he could see. Up close, they were frightening. However, Red Eagle's attention was drawn to the horses, some being ridden, others tied to the wagons. He was determined to take one of them.

Another horseman came riding back from the wagon train.

Red Eagle peered through the bushes. The horseman stopped and waved to the man on the sorrel to join him. The two rode back to the wagons.

For the next two hours, Red Eagle watched the wagon train, wondering why it had stopped. He was getting out a piece of meat to chew on when he heard a commotion coming from the wagon train. Men yelling, wagons moving. Red Eagle thought they were leaving, but instead, they formed a large circle. He watched as teams of mules and oxen were unhitched from the wagons, and along with many of the horses, herded outside of the circle to graze.

Red Eagle studied the horses and decided to approach them in the early morning hours, but just before dark, men drove the animals back inside the circle of wagons.

Small campfires lit up the area, and the aroma of cooking food drifted back to Red Eagle. He knew taking a horse was impossible, but maybe he could get some of the food. He had watched the women take foodstuff from barrels and wooden boxes mounted on the sides of the wagons. Red Eagle drank all the water he could hold, knowing it would cause him to wake up in a few hours.

While Red Eagle was being tormented by the smell of hot food. Andy Moorehouse, along with Luke and Jake, sat drinking coffee while Dave Daggett gave them his scouting report.

"And you didn't see nothin'?" asked Luke.

"Nothin' but that dust cloud northwest of the canyon. That's why I was so late gettin' back."

"More'n likely a dust devil," said Moorehouse. "Just the same, I want you up there in the mornin' at sunup. We'll pull outta here at first light." Then he turned to Emmett. "Pass the word; everyone sleeps inside the circle tonight. Check with the guards; tell 'em to stay alert, I don't want no damned lollygaggin' this close to Cobble Canyon."

As Daggett turned to leave, Moorehouse said, "Be careful out there tomorrow, Dave, If something don't seem right, you hightail it back here."

"Sure, Andy."

"I mean it, Dave. Don't be a hero."

CHAPTER THREE

Red Eagle awoke from a bad dream. He had dreamed he was going home, sitting astride one of the mules pulling a wagon he had taken from the outsiders. It was loaded with all sorts of clothing and food. His tribe would be proud of him, but when he started across the river, his people began throwing rocks and shouting, "Go away. Outsiders are not welcome."

He rubbed the sleep from his eyes; looked at the moon and judged there to be at least three more hours of darkness. He rolled up the blanket and stashed it, along with the water skin in a clump of sagebrush. Then, with the leather pouch slung over his shoulder, he set out for the wagons.

Unknown to Red Eagle, he could not have picked a worse time to approach the wagons, what with the extra guards and a full moon that lit up the prairie, taking away what little concealment there was. Bent low in a crouch, he slowly approached the wagons. Suddenly, a match flared as one of the guards lit up a smoking pipe. Red Eagle was less than thirty yards away and could see the man's face clearly, a round face with a black beard. Lucky for Red Eagle, the guard had chosen that particular time to light up. It warned Red Eagle and ruined the guard's night vision. Moving to his left, he spotted another guard. Red Eagle lay on his stomach, watching, trying to decide what to do. The guard strolled down the line of wagons and joined the man smoking the pipe. Red Eagle could hear them talking. He crept up to the wagon the guard had just left. Mounted on the side were two long wooden boxes secured with leather straps. Rising to his knees, Red Eagle cut the straps with Gray Cloud's knife. The lid wouldn't open. He ran his hand along the top of the box and found a metal hasp. A bent nail hung through a metal hook. He removed the nail and slowly opened the lid. Reaching inside, he felt meat, covered with salt. Red Eagle began slicing off slabs of meat, and stuffing them into his leather pouch.

Charlie Tippon had had another fight with his wife, Clara. It seemed the farther west they traveled, the more cantankerous she became. He knew she hadn't been crazy about leaving Missouri, but Charlie thought she had accepted his argument about living where there was no winter and where a man could raise two crops a year. Nevertheless, the longer they were on the trail, the grander that old Missouri farm grew in her mind. That night after supper, Clara started complaining again about leaving a wonderful farm behind and traveling through dangerous Indian country to some Godforsaken place that neither one of them knew anything about. Charlie lost his temper. "Gawdalmightydamn," he shouted, "what wonderful farm? A two room shack sittin' on a forty acre rock pile?" He grabbed a blanket and left the campfire. After smoking a pipe full of tobacco, he crawled under the wagon; rolled up in his blanket and fell asleep.

In the early morning hours, something awoke Charlie. He

pulled the blanket away from his face and saw movement beside the wagon. "Hey!" he yelled, sticking his head out from under the wagon, "who's there?"

Red Eagle brought the butt end of the knife down hard on poor old Charlie's baldhead. At the same time, the box lid slammed shut with a loud thud.

The two guards, Joe Perkins and Otis Potter, heard the commotion and ran for the wagon. Otis fired his rifle in the air to alert everyone.

Red Eagle dove under the wagon and began crawling on all fours. He scrambled under the wagon behind Charlie's and then on to the next wagon. He could hear people yelling. Red Eagle spang to his feet and started running.

People on the wagon train were jarred awake by the rifle shot. They threw their blankets aside and grabbed their weapons. Amid the confusion, Andy Moorehouse's booming voice could be heard shouting orders. "Women and children to the center of the circle. The rest of you take your places between the wagons. Hold your fire 'less you see somethin'."

Dawn was breaking and there was just enough daylight to allow Joe Perkins to spot Red Eagle. Perkins dropped to a kneeling position, took aim and fired.

Red Eagle's right leg was knocked from under him. He thought he had stumbled, and scrambled to his feet, but his leg collapsed. As he fell, a cracking noise sounded above his head. He struggled to rise, but a booted foot shoved down hard on the back of his neck. Red Eagle still held the knife in his hand and thrust it behind him, catching Perkins in the calf of the leg.

Perkins let out a yelp and brought the rifle butt down hard on Red Eagle's head. More men showed up "Are you okay Joe?" someone asked.

"Yeah, I'm awright, but I need some help. He knifed me in the leg."

"The sonofabitch," the man said and swung his rifle around.

"Don't shoot him," yelled Perkins. "We've gotta find out what he's doin' here."

Perkins draped his arms around two men's shoulders and they headed back to the wagons. Two other men dragged Red Eagle by his feet. When they were back inside the circle of wagons, a crowd gathered around.

"Someone get Ellie Addison," Andy Moorehouse yelled, "tell her we've got wounded people here." He searched Red Eagle's pouch. Looking up at Daggett he said, "He was stealin' food."

Charlie Tippon pushed his way through the crowd, hollering, "Get outta my way, I wanna see the Injun what tried to scalp me." He looked down at Red Eagle, then at Moorehouse. "The bastard tried to scalp me, Andy."

Moorehouse started laughing. "C'mon Charlie, the only thing he scalped was your salt pork."

"I don't see what's so damned funny," said Frank Ortman. "He could be a scout for a war party."

"He's no scout," said Moorehouse. "He was after food."

"That's what you say," said Ortman. "Well that ain't good enough." Then, he kicked Red Eagle in the ribs. Moorehouse's fist caught Ortman flush on the jaw, sending him sprawling. He scrambled to his feet with a knife in his hand. Daggett pulled his pistol and said, "Drop the knife." Ortman took a step forward. Daggett thumbed back the pistol hammer.

"Stop it," Ellie Addison screamed, elbowing her way through the crowd. "I don't need any more patients." Ortman glared at Moorehouse and Daggett, then stuck the knife in his waistband and stalked off.

"Now," said Ellie "all of you get out of my way and let me look at this man."

"Okay, folks," shouted Moorehouse, "the show's over. Back to your wagons." He turned to Ellie Addison and said, "Joe Perkins was stabbed in the leg."

"I've already taken care of Joe. Where's this one shot?"

"In the back of the right leg," said Daggett.

"Well, don't stand there. Turn him over."

Moorehouse left Harrison Giles, his supply wagon driver, and Nate Williams, with Ellie Addison. "When Ellie's through workin' on the Indian, tie him in the wagon. Nate, you ride with Giles, and keep an eye on the Indian."

"Aw hell, Andy, you can't expect me to ride in that damned wagon."

"The hell I can't."

"But them danged things'll jar a man's kidneys loose."

"If the Indian can stand it, so can you," said Moorehouse. Then he turned to Daggett, "C'mon, we've wasted enough time. You head on out to Cobble Canyon for a look see. I've gotta get this train movin'."

"What about the Indian? Whatta you aimin' to do with him?"

"Dammit, I don't know, depends on what kinda shape he's in come evenin'."

"Hell, your problem's solved," said Daggett, "if the wagon ride don't kill him, poor old Nate probably will." Daggett started to ride off, then turned back. "Andy, keep a close watch on Ortman. He's a mean one."

"He's a pain in the ass is what he is. I'm kickin' him loose when we get to Fort Laramie."

CHAPTER FOUR

Daggett rode hard for Cobble Canyon. He had lost an hour and a half with all the commotion back at the wagon train. A mile short of the canyon he reined in his horse to a slow walk. He wanted it rested when he got there.

As he neared the canyon, shots rang out. Daggett jerked his rifle from the saddle scabbard, leapt from his horse and crept to the rim of the canyon. Below on the far side, two men hunkered down behind an overturned wagon. A half dozen Indians had them pinned down. The Indians were on Daggett's side of the canyon with their backs to him. He took out his pistol and laid it beside him, picked up the rifle and fired into a rock over their heads. Then he grabbed up the pistol and emptied it in their direction. Then he ducked out of sight and reloaded.

The gunfire in the canyon stopped. Daggett heard the pounding of horse hoofs and a lot of yelling. The Indians were beating a retreat. He stood up and fired twice more over their heads. They had been caught in a crossfire, and had no idea how many people they were dealing with. He watched the Indians disappear around a bend in the canyon. Daggett stood up and waved his rifle over his head at the men below. They waved back. He got on his horse and started down the canyon trail. The two men were unhitching a dead mule from the wagon. The other mule had been shot, and was still down. Daggett rode up to them and dismounted. The two of them were a grubby looking pair. One was a large bald man with a full red beard. The other, a scrawny hatchet faced fellow with long stringy blonde hair. The big one walked over to Daggett with his hand out. "Names Roth, Jeff Roth." He nodded to the other man. "This here's my partner, Ernie Ledbetter. I don't know who you are, or what you're doin' here Mister, but we shore are beholdin' to you."

"Name's Dave Daggett. I'm scoutin' for a wagon train." Then motioning to a pile of buffalo hides that had spilled out of the overturned wagon, he said, "Guess I don't have to ask why those Indians were after you two."

"Hey," said Ledbetter, "It's not like we're wipin' out their herds. We take jest enough to make a decent livin'."

"Yeah, you and a few hundred others."

Roth broke in. "You said you're scoutin' fer a wagon train. Think yer boss'd mind

if we rode along with you fer a ways?"

"I reckon not, you'd have to ask him though. But what about your wagon and hides?"

"If he'd loan us a couple a mules, we'd pay him. You think he'd do that?"

"I don't know. Like I said, you'll have to ask him." Daggett looked at the wounded mule. "What about your animal? You gonna put it down?" Ledbetter walked over and shot the mule behind the ear.

Daggett knew he should go back and let Moorehouse know what had taken place. But he wanted to make sure the Indians had cleared the canyon. He looked the two buffalo hunters over and said, "Wait atop the canyon for the wagon train, it should be comin' along soon. Tell 'em what happened here. They'll give you a hand with your wagon. I should be back in a couple of hours." Daggett jerked his horse around and rode off down the canyon trail.

As the wagon train approached Cobble Canyon, Moorehouse spotted the two buffalo hunters. He stopped the train and motioned for his two outriders, Jake Vines and Luke Norton to join him.

"What's the problem?" asked Luke.

Moorehouse nodded toward the canyon. "Two men, there on the canyon rim."

Jake shaded his eyes. "Where's their mounts?"

"That's what we aim to find out," said Moorehouse. The three rode out to meet the two strangers. When they were about a hundred yards away, Moorehouse reined his horse to a stop. "Spread out," he ordered Luke and Jake. "Get some distance between us, and be alert."

Flanked by Jake and Luke, Moorehouse rode up to the two men. "Whatta you doin' out here on foot?" he asked.

"Induns jumped us," said Roth. "Our wagons turned over in the canyon. They killed one of our mules. We had to shoot the other one."

Moorehouse slid off his horse and looked in the canyon. "Dammit, how long ago'd this happen? I had a scout out here."

"Couple hours ago," said Roth. "But your scout is okay. If it hadn't been fer him comin' along when he did, those Induns woulda done us in fer sure. He run 'em off."

"He followed them?" asked Moorehouse.

"Yeah, you oughta seen 'em hightailin' it on up the canyon."

Moorehouse turned to Luke and Jake. "Ride after Dave, he might need some help." Then he turned back to the buffalo hunters.

"You didn't have horses?"

"One," said Ledbetter, "but it bolted when the shootin' started."

"You two stay put. I'll get you some help with your wagon, then we'll try to find your horse."

Red Eagle awoke sitting on the floor of a wagon, surrounded by barrels, boxes and large burlap bags. He tried to move, and realized his wrists were tied to the side of the wagon. His head ached, and his right leg and ribs hurt. The jostling of the wagon caused him to moan in pain.

Nate Williams swung his feet over the back of the wagon seat and faced Red Eagle. "Well, well," he said, "look who's awake. I was kinda hopin' you'd do us all a favor and give up the ghost."

Red Eagle couldn't understand the man, and jerked at his bonds.

"Easy," said Williams, "We'll soon be to Cobble Canyon, and if'n I'm lucky, maybe Andy Moorehouse'll set you loose there. I hope so, 'cause I'm sure as hell tired ridin' this wagon."

Moorehouse rode back to the wagon train and sent a half dozen men to help the buffalo hunters, then headed for the supply wagon.

When Moorehouse rode up, Nate Williams was standing next to the wagon rolling a cigarette. "I thought I told you to stay in the wagon with the Indian," Moorehouse said.

"Hell, Andy, he ain't goin' nowhere."
"Where's Red?"
"He went to get some coffee."
"How's the Indian doin'?"
"He ain't dead."
"Go fetch Ellie. I'll keep an eye on him."

Moorehouse climbed into the wagon. He and Red Eagle stared at each other. Moorehouse took out a knife and reached over to cut him loose. Red Eagle's eyes widened, and he began struggling. Moorehouse put the knife away, and pointed at the ropes. Red Eagle relaxed, and Moorehouse untied him.

"C'mon," Moorehouse said, and motioned for Red Eagle to get out of the wagon. Red Eagle grabbed the sides and pulled himself up onto his knees. The pain was great, not so much from the wound, as from being in a sitting position for so long. Moorehouse jumped down and stood by the front wheel, motioning for Red Eagle to follow. Red Eagle swung his legs over the side, and placed his feet on the wheel spokes. Moorehouse reached around his waist and helped him down. Red Eagle crawled over and sat with his back against the wagon wheel. Moorehouse stared at him, wondering what to do.

Nate Williams showed up with Ellie. "What's he doing out of the wagon?" Ellie asked.

"C'mon, Ellie, you don't think I'm gonna haul him all the way to California, do you?"

"You're a hard man, Andy Moorehouse, but even you can't leave this boy out here alone, the shape he's in."

"Well, what in the world do you expect me to do?"

"I expect you to keep him with this train until he's strong enough to sit a horse."

"He ain't got no horse."

"I'm sure you'll figure something out. Now, get him undressed so I can examine him."

"Dang it, Ellie, I ain't go..."

"Enough," shouted Ellie. "We'll talk about this later."

When they tried to undress Red Eagle, he put up a fight. Finally, Ellie shouted, "Hold it, you're hurting him. Just bare his leg so I can look at the wound."

Ellie examined Red Eagle as best she could, cleaned the wound and changed the dressing on his leg. "Now," she said, "help him back in the wagon, and don't tie him up."

Moorehouse started to protest, but decided to let it be. "How's he doin'?" he asked.

"He's got some sore ribs, but his leg wound is coming along okay. Barring infection, I'd say he'll be up and about in three or four days. He's young and strong, he'll mend fast."

Williams muttered, "Not fast enough, as far as...." but stopped in mid sentence when he caught Ellie's scornful look.

"I'd still like to know what he's doin' out here by himself," said Moorehouse.

"We'll probably never know," Ellie said, turning to leave. "I'll check on him tomorrow,"

Williams frowned. "Andy, I don't cotton ridin' with this Indian, and him untied. I don't trust him."

"Well, then you'll just have to keep a close eye on him, won't you."

"Another thing," said Williams, "I can't ride this damned wagon for three or four more days either, not with Giles. The guy never talks."

"Dammit, Nate, quit your whinin'. You're just gonna have to bear it, besides, you talk enough for the both of you. Now, I've gotta get this train movin'." He rode off leaving Williams muttering to himself.

Moorehouse rode back to the canyon. The buffalo hunters wagon had been turned upright. He spotted Daggett, standing next to it, talking to Luke and Jake. He spurred his horse down the canyon trail.

"Can I talk to you a minute?" asked Roth, as Moorehouse rode past.

"Not now," said Moorehouse, and waved Daggett over.

"The Indians are long gone," Daggett said, "but we ought not waste any more time."

"Okay," said Moorehouse, "take Jake with you and ride on ahead. Luke, go and bring the wagons on up." Then, he turned back to Roth and said, "I suppose you're wantin' to borrow a couple of mules? Well, I ain't got any."

"Hell, I'll pay for the use of the mules if someone would just let me borrow 'em 'til we get to where I can pick up a pair. Look Mister, I can't leave my wagon and hides."

Moorehouse looked around and yelled to a man named Roberts. "Go back to the wagons. See if you can find someone who's willin' to rent some mules or oxen for a few days."

"Much obliged," said Roth. "We'll earn our way, and if there's any Indun trouble, you'll have two more guns."

"The same two guns that lost your mules in the first place?" said Moorehouse, and started to ride off.

"Another thing," Roth shouted, "my partner, Ernie, speaks this Indun lingo. That might come in handy."

Moorehouse whirled his horse around. "You speak Indian?" he asked.

"Shore do," said Ledbetter, "if'n they're Cheyenne."

Moorehouse studied Ledbetter a minute, and said, "Look me up later, I might have a job for you."

CHAPTER FIVE

Ellie watched Red Eagle as he leaned against the wagon wheel eating the stew she had brought to him and Nate Williams. Red Eagle had heard about tribes with women healers but had never seen one. She handed him a canteen of water. He took a drink and handed it back, but Ellie motioned him to keep it.

Andy Moorehouse showed up with Ledbetter. "Who's this?" asked Ellie nodding at the stranger.

"His name's Ledbetter, he speaks Indian. I aim to find out what this Indian's doin' out here all by hisself."

"I'd like to know myself," Ellie said.

"Yeah, me too," Nate Williams chimed in.

"Nate," said Moorehouse, "why don't you go get a cup of coffee."

"I don't like Cookie's coffee."

"Well dammit, go get something you do like."

Nate walked away mumbling to himself.

Moorehouse turned to Ledbetter, "Okay, let's start with his name."

Ledbetter asked Red Eagle his name. Red Eagle stood staring at this yellow haired stranger who spoke his language.

"Must not be Cheyenne, he don't seem to understand what I asked him."

"My name is Red Eagle, son of Gray Wolf."

"Well, I'll be damned, He is Cheyenne, says his name's Red Eagle."

"Ask him what he's doin' out here alone," said Moorehouse.

Ledbetter and Red Eagle spoke for several minutes before Moorehouse grew impatient and broke in. "Well, what the hell is he sayin'?"

"He wants to know where the faraway place is that we're headin fer. Says he can't go back home, so he's gonna follow the wagons to that faraway place."

"Why can't he go back home?" Ellie asked.

"I don't know, he won't tell me, just says he shamed hisself and family."

"Musta been somethin' pretty bad," said Moorehouse.

Ledbetter looked at Red Eagle and back at Moorehouse. "To him maybe, but maybe not to us."

"Whatta you talkin' about?" asked Moorehouse,

"Indians are a funny lot," said Ledbetter. "They figure anything goes when they're dealin' with the white man or another tribe, but they hold their own to a strict set a rules. Hell, he might've done nothin' more'n sass an elder. He could've took more'n his share after a hunt, or didn't mind his daddy. Something we wouldn't give a second thought to."

"I'd still like to know what he done," said Moorehouse.

Ledbetter spoke again to Red Eagle. "Ain't no use," said Ledbetter, "he won't tell me."

"Ask him," said Ellie, "if he has any friends at all nearby."

The two spoke again. "He ain't got no friends," said Ledbetter. "He's determined to see the faraway place that we're headin' fer."

"Well, that ain't gonna happen," said Moorehouse and stomped off.

Ellie spoke up. "Tell me, Mr. Ledbetter, can you teach Red Eagle English?"

"Shore," said Ledbetter, then grinned and said, "a lot easier than I could teach you Cheyenne."

"How long would it take you?"

"Depends."

"Depends on what?"

"Oh, how much time I spend with him, and how willin' he is to learn."

"If he cooperates, how long?"

"I reckon I could have him speakin' passable English in a month or so. Why?"

Ellie ignored his question and asked, "Would you teach him if he's willing to learn?"

"Afraid I ain't gonna be with this train that long ma'am. You see, my partner and me is havin' to rent a team of mules, and it's costin' us money, so we'll be leavin' the train as soon as we can."

"What happened to your animals?"

"Indians killed 'em."

"How much are you paying for the team you have now?"

"Too damned much." Said Ledbetter. He looked away and then back at Ellie. "Sorry ma'am, but I get mad when I think of payin' out a quarter a day. That's a heap of money, but what choice we got?"

Red Eagle stood silently, studying the faces of Ellie and

Ledbetter. He knew they were talking about him.

Ellie walked over and took the empty bowl from Red Eagle. Then she turned back to Ledbetter and said, "I'll make you a deal, Mr. Ledbetter. You spend the rest of the time you're with the wagon train teaching this young man English, and I'll pay half the rental cost of the mules. Of course, that's if he's willing to learn."

"Why would you wanna do that?"

"Is it a deal or not?"

Ledbetter thought a minute, and said, "He'd have to do some work," then added, "that is, when he's able."

"That goes without saying."

Ledbetter looked at Red Eagle and back at Ellie. "Okay, it's a deal."

"Good, now take the boy with you, You'll be responsible for him. I'll cook the evening meals for you, the boy and your partner."

"That seems more'n fair to me. I'm all fer it, but what if my partner don't go along with it?"

"Then let your partner…What's his name?"

"Jeff Roth."

"Then let Mr. Roth pay for the mules and do his own cooking. That is, if you two have anything to cook."

Ledbetter shoved his hands deep into his pockets then turned and spoke to Red Eagle. Red Eagle's eyes widened. He stared at Ellie and said something to Ledbetter.

"Well, what's it going to be?" asked Ellie.

"I explained it all to him, and he's eager to learn. But I don't know. Even if my partner goes along with it, what about Andy Moorehouse. He ain't gonna like it."

"Let me worry about Andy Moorehouse. Now, go along, and take the boy with you."

"Okay, I'll take him, but I ain't promisin' nothin', so don't get mad if I bring him back."

"If it doesn't work out," said Ellie, "you don't bring him back. You hunt down Nate Williams and turn the boy over to him. You understand?"

"Yes ma'am."

Ellie stood hands on hips, watching Red Eagle limping alongside Ledbetter. After a short distance Ledbetter put his arm around Red Eagle's waist to help support him. This gesture of kindness made Ellie look on the unkempt buffalo hunter in a different light.

She thought of her son, Aaron, who would be about the same age as Red Eagle, had he lived, He died at the age of twelve with peritonitis when his appendix ruptured. Even though Ellie was a physician, there was no way to stem the deadly infection. A short time later her husband passed away and she decided to start over as far away from Baltimore as she could get. As a female, her male associates had never accepted her. Even the nurses resented taking orders from her. And the patients seemed uncomfortable being treated by a female doctor. Some of them actually refused to be treated by a woman. Therefore, Ellie had been nothing more than a glorified nurse, assigned menial tasks.

When Ellie read a newspaper article about the westward migration, she packed her things and bought a train ticket to St, Louis. She figured in an unsettled land people couldn't be so choosy about the gender of their doctor. From St. Louis she made her way to Independence where she bought a wagon, a team of mules and supplies, then made a deal with Andy Moorehouse: In return for free passage she would provide free medical care for all, minus the cost of the medicine. Ellie figured this would be a great opportunity, a chance to prove to others that she was a good doctor. If she cared for the families on the journey, then, surely they would accept her when they reached their destination. She would build her practice on the trail west.

Ellie was gathering the soup bowls when Nate Williams showed up followed by Moorehouse.

"Where's the Indian? In the wagon?" asked Moorehouse.

Ellie was busy wiping out the bowls with dead grass. "No" she answered.

"No, whatta you mean no?"

"He's traveling with the two buffalo hunters now."

"What?"

"Well, you didn't want to be bothered with him, so now you don't have to. They agreed to take him. Seems like a good idea to me."

"Me too," chimed in Nate.

Moorehouse gave Nate a hard look. Then turned back to Ellie. "Now, I wonder why they'd wanna do that?"

Ellie set the bowls aside. "It seems the boy wants to learn English, so in return for whatever work he can do, Mr. Ledbetter is going to give him English lessons."

Moorehouse took off his hat, examined the headband, and put it back on. "I don't suppose you had anything to do with this?"

"It may have come up when I was talking to Mr. Ledbetter. Yes, I'm sure it did."

CHAPTER SIX

Red Eagle was a good student. After three days he had learned many phrases, one of the first he had learned from Ledbetter was, "No, dammit, no."

Ledbetter would say to Red Eagle in Cheyenne, "Where is the river?" Red Eagle might say, "When is the river?" Then he'd quickly correct himself by shouting, "NO, DAMMIT, NO...WHERE IS THE RIVER?"

Jeff Roth didn't like Ledbetter spending so much time with Red Eagle, but with Ellie paying half the mule rental and cooking their supper, he put up with it, although he still grumbled about having to wait until she had finished her evening rounds before eating.

Sarah and Charlotte Ortman, were ten and fourteen years old, ages when curiosity outweighs judgement. The sisters had heard some hair-raising stories about Indians and wanted to sneak a peek at the Indian, Red Eagle. They were walking along the circle of wagons one evening, and as they approached the buffalo hunters' wagon, Sarah said, "Maybe we'd better turn back. Papa told us to stay clear of the Indian's wagon."

Charlotte, the eldest, said, "We're only passing by. Besides, I want to look at the Indian, don't you?"

"Yeah, but what if Papa finds out?"

"He won't find out. Now, C'mon, fraidy cat."

Ledbetter and Red Eagle sat on the ground, their backs against the wagon wheel. Red Eagle was concentrating on some new words he had been taught, and Ledbetter was smoking a cigarette. Red Eagle watched Ledbetter puffing away. "Why that you do?" he asked.

"Do what?"

"Put fire in mouth."

"It's not fire, dammit. It's tobacco burnin'."

Red Eagle switched to Cheyenne. "My people do that, but not with paper, and only for special times."

"Dammit," said Ledbetter, "I told you not to be speakin' Cheyenne. You got to think in American."

Red Eagle sat watching Ledbetter. "I try."

"You don't try. You gotta do it. You gotta think all the time in American."

"No," said Red Eagle, holding out his hand, "I try tobacco."

Ledbetter laughed. "No, you can't."

"Why?"

"'Cause it'll stunt your growth."

Red Eagle looked puzzled. "What stunt?"

"You won't grow. You'll always stay little."

"You stay little. You stunt?"

Ledbetter shook his head. "I take after my Pappy. He was little. Everyone called him the little Leprechaun."

"Leprechaun? What is Leprechaun?"

It's an Irish little person."

"What is Irish?"

Ledbetter glared at Red Eagle. "It's someone from Ireland."

Red Eagle stared at Ledbetter, then looked away. "What is Ireland?"

"Dammit, it's a country. Like this country, only greener."

"You been there?"

"No I ain't been there, but my Pappy was born there. He told me that it's the most purttiest place in the world, with green grass year round, purty fences made just by stackin' rocks. But the best thing about Ireland, he said was the singin' and the beer. Said it was the best-damned beer in the whole wide world. In fact, he..." At that moment Ledbetter saw Charlotte and Sarah coming their way. He watched the two girls approaching and nudged Red Eagle. "When those two girls get next to the wagon I want you to stand up, and in English, say, 'You got pretty hair.'"

Red Eagle kept repeating the phrase "You got pretty hair."

Sarah was scared, but forced herself to look at Red Eagle. His difference in appearance: the way he was dressed, and the long hair frightened her. She clung tightly to Charlotte.

When the two girls neared the wagon, Red Eagle stared at Charlotte, and she stared back. He couldn't get over her beautiful yellow hair.

Ledbetter poked Red Eagle with his elbow, and whispered, "You got pretty hair."

Startled, Red Eagle sprang to his feet and yelled, "Pretty hair."

Sarah jerked loose from Charlotte and took off running and screaming, "Help, help, he's gonna scalp us."

Charlotte chased after her, yelling for her to stop. Everyone turned to see what the commotion was all about. Charlotte finally caught up to her sister, and grabbed her by the shoulders. "You're being silly, now, be quiet. Everyone's looking at us."

Red Eagle was confused, wondering why the girls ran away scared, and why his friend Ledbetter was laughing

"What I say?" Red Eagle asked.

"It's not what you said," laughed Ledbetter. "It's what them girls thought you said."

Jeff Roth came from behind the wagon. "What the hell's goin' on?" he yelled.

Ledbetter stopped laughing. "Nothin'. Red Eagle said somethin' about them gal's hair and they got scared, that's all."

"Gawddammit, I told you that Indun was gonna be trouble. Did you put him up to it?"

"Hell, Jeff, I was just havin' a little fun. Ain't no reason to get all worked up."

"I ain't worked up, but might be some of these folks won't think it's as funny as you do. Dammit, he's an Indun."

Ledbetter's face grew somber. "So's my wife, remember?"

"You know what I mean, dammit. These folks ain't like you and me. They're....they....Aw, to hell with it," he said and walked away.

Frank Ortman heard all the noise, and was on his way to see what the ruckus was about. His daughter Sarah came running up to him. "Papa, Papa, that Indian scared me."

"What?"

"It was nothing," said Charlotte, "really, Papa. She got scared over nothing."

Ortman stared at his daughter. "I told you to stay away from that Indian. Now, you two go on back to our wagon."

"But Papa," cried Charlotte, "nothing...."

"Go back to the wagon. Now!"

Ledbetter spotted Ortman hurrying toward him, with a group of people following behind. He turned to Red Eagle. "Go check on the mules."

"What?"

"I said go look after the mules. Now! And stay there 'til I come after you."

Puzzled, Red Eagle left.

Ledbetter took out his knife and began whittling on a piece of wood.

Ortman strode up and stood in front of Ledbetter. "Which one are you? Roth or Ledbetter?"

"Name's Ledbetter. Who are you?"

"Where's the Indian?"

Ledbetter kept up his whittling, and without looking up, asked, "Who wants to know?"

"I do, by God."

"And who are you?"

"My name is Frank Ortman. Now, where's the Indian?"

"You wanna see him for any particular reason?"

"Look," said Ortman, "that Indian did or said something to my two girls, and I want to know what it was."

"It weren't nothin'," said Ledbetter.

I'll decide that. Now, where's the Indian?"

"He's out huntin'."

"Well, then you shouldn't mind if I take a look around," said Ortman, and turned toward the wagon.

Ledbetter sprang to his feet, knife in hand. "You callin' me a liar Mister?"

"Just then, Jeff Roth, walked up. "What's the problem here?"

Ortman whirled around and looked the newcomer over. "Are you Roth?"

"That's right. Now, what's goin' on here?"

Ortman looked at Ledbetter and back at Roth. "I'm looking for the Indian. Your friend here tells me he's out hunting. Well, I don't believe him. I want to look in your wagon."

Roth's face reddened. He walked over to Ortman, dwarfing the smaller man. "First off," he said, "if my partner says the Indun ain't here, he ain't here, and they ain't nobody gonna look in my wagon."

Ortman's gaze went from Roth to Ledbetter, to the wagon and back to Roth. "This isn't over," he said, "I aim to talk to the Indian." He spun around and pushed his way through the crowd yelling, "Out of my way."

Roth watched Ortman leave, then turned on Ledbetter. "Well, you've gone and spilt the milk this time," he shouted. "Your little fun games is gonna windup gettin' someone hurt."

"Aw, Jeff, I told ya nothin' happened. That old man's crazy."

"That may well be, but a stunt like you pulled could very well get us kicked off this train. Then what the hell we gonna do stuck out here on the prairie with a wagonload of skins and no mules? Let's jest hope none've what happened here gets back to Andy Moorehouse. Roth looked around. "Now, where's the Indun?"

"He's with the mules."

"Go get him. And for the rest of the time we're with this outfit you're not to let him outta your sight. You understand?"

"Hell, Jeff, I onl…"

"Go get the Indun," Roth yelled.

Ledbetter didn't like being ordered around but said nothing because he knew Roth was right. He also knew this wasn't the time to argue with the big man.

For the next few days, Roth and Ledbetter walked on eggshells. They stuck close to their wagon and kept Red Eagle out of sight. On the fourth day Ledbetter figured Andy Moorehouse hadn't heard about the incident with Frank Ortman, but Roth wasn't convinced. "I can't stand this not knowin'," he told Ledbetter. "I'm goin' up and talk to him."

"Hold on," said Ledbetter, "I don't think that's such a good idea. He ain't said nothin', and you might jest stir somethin' up. Best leave sleepin' dogs lie."

"To hell with sleepin' dogs. I can't stand not knowin'. Don't worry, if he don't say anything about what happened I wont either." Roth turned and walked away.

"Don't make no damned sense what you're doin'" yelled Ledbetter.

Roth stopped, and pointed a finger at Ledbetter. "You jest better remember who started all this ruckus."

Roth didn't have a mount and had to walk, making sure he gave the Ortman wagon a wide berth. The wagons had stopped, and as Roth neared the head of the column, he saw Moorehouse up ahead talking to his scout, Dave Daggett. He hurried up and joined them, "Howdy," he said.

The two men nodded to him. Then Moorehouse turned back to Daggett. "How bad is it?"

"Not good," said Daggett," but I found a place 'bout a quarter of a mile downstream that looks fordable. Water's a little swift, but it ain't all that deep."

"Always somethin', huh?" put in Roth, feeling awkward, standing there while the other men talked.

Daggett looked at him and said, "River's up some," he said, "must've had a downpour up north of here."

"What choices we got?" asked Moorehouse.

"Well," said Daggett, looking back toward the river, "I could take a look farther downstream but ain't no guarantee I'd find a better place. More'n likely it'd be a waste of time, so that leaves us with two choices, either cross now, or wait 'til the river goes down, and that'd cost us at least two days."

Moorehouse took off his hat and wiped the sweatband with his kerchief. "We'll take a look," he said to Daggett then turned to Roth. "Wanna come along?"

Moorehouse's offer surprised Roth. "I ain't got no mount."

Moorehouse kicked a foot out of the stirrup and offered his hand. Roth stuck his foot in the empty stirrup and swung up behind him.

Roth could hear the river long before he saw it. The place Daggett had picked to make the crossing was about fifty feet wide. The rushing water was swift and shut out all other sounds, but the rapids showed it was fairly shallow.

"Well, whatta you think?" Daggett yelled over the water's roar.

"I'd say no more'n three feet deep, four at the most," Moorehouse yelled back. "Whatta you think?"

"About that," shouted Daggett.

Moorehouse spurred his horse away from the river. When the river noise was behind them he reined up and they dismounted.

Moorehouse began tightening the saddle cinch. He looked across the horse's rump where Roth stood and said, "The place Dave picked out looks promisin'. How would you feel about goin' first, leadin' the way? That buffalo wagon of yours has got extra large wheels with wide rims. You could sorta test the waters so to speak."

Roth thought a minute about what Moorehouse suggested. "Now I see why you two invited me along."

"Well, whatta you say?" asked Moorehouse.

Roth stood looking at the river. "I reckon I owe you two guys, but I'd have to unload my buffalo hides. Wouldn't wanna lose 'em."

"No, I think you'd best leave 'em in the wagon," said Moorehouse, "the more weight, the less the water's gonna push you around."

"Wait a minute," said Roth, "even with my wagon's big wheels and weighted down, if I make it across that don't mean them other wagons will."

"Yeah, but if you don't make it," grinned Daggett, "then we'll know the other wagons won't ether."

Roth smiled at Daggett's humor. He knew Ledbetter was gonna raise hell. "My partner's gonna scream to high heaven," he said, "specially 'bout leavin' the hides in the wagon."

Moorehouse and Daggett stood staring at him.

"Okay," said Roth, "I'll do it."

"Good," said Moorehouse, "I appreciate it. We'll camp where the wagons are tonight, First thing in the mornin' bring your wagon to the front of the column."

CHAPTER SEVEN

The buffalo hunters' wagon led the column to the river with Ledbetter griping all the way. Red Eagle sat on the skins directly behind the seat, holding on to one side of the wagon like he was told.

"What the hell got into you anyway?" Ledbetter yelled. "Volunteerin' us to cross the river first and with our buffalo skins in the wagon to boot. Gawddammit we ain't part of this train."

"Oh, hush yore damned yammerin'," yelled Roth. "You fergettin' if it weren't fer Daggett and this here wagon train we wouldn't be worryin' about no river right now. Besides, what with yore little fun and games back there with the Indun, I was afraid not to do what he asked me."

Andy Moorehouse stopped the column and rode over to the buffalo hunters' wagon. "Which one of you'll be takin' the wagon across? No need for both of you to go."

"Well," said Roth, "Ernie here's a better muleskinner than me."

Ledbetter spoke up. "We'll both go. I might need some help."

"Suit yourself," said Moorehouse. Then spotting Red Eagle in the back, he said, "Hold on. You can't cross with him in the back. Hell, if something happened he'd be a goner."

"Well, how's he supposed to cross over?" said Roth.

"Hell, he can ride with someone that might need some help. Now tell him to get outta there."

Ledbetter spoke to Red Eagle in Cheyenne, and he climbed out.

"Okay," said Moorehouse, "follow Dave. He'll show you where to commence your crossin'."

Daggett led the wagon down to the water's edge. "Now, start your crossin' headin' a little upstream 'cause the currents gonna try movin' you the other way, and whatever you do don't stop. If them mules start slowin' down don't let 'em, even if you have to get out on the wagon tongue and kick 'em in the butt."

"You through?" asked Ledbetter.

"Yeah. Good luck."

Ledbetter turned to Roth, "Now if the mules start actin' up, yer job's to get out there and keep 'em movin'."

"Dammit, Ernie, yore lighter and more nimble than me. Might be better if…"

"No, no," interrupted Ledbetter. "I gotta stay put. I'm a better muleskinner than you are. Remember?"

"Ernie."

"What?"

"I can't swim."

"You shoulda thought about that before volunteerin' us." Ledbetter pulled his hat down hard on his head and started whipping the mules and yelling. The mules plowed into the water. Roth reeled backward, grabbed the bottom of the seat with both hands and held on tight. The rushing water slammed into the side of the wagon. The two men disappeared in a watery spray. One mule lost its footing and almost went down. Roth gripped the seat so hard his fingers ached. "Keep 'em movin' Ernie. Oh for God sake keep 'em movin'." The mules jumped and lunged about, fighting the current but steadily moved ahead. After what seemed much longer than the three or so minutes it took to cross, it was over. The wagon reached shallow water. Ledbetter whipped the mules up the far bank. The two men sat in silence, soaking wet. Roth turned to Ledbetter. "Now see, that weren't so bad, huh?" Ledbetter gave him a wry look and climbed down to check the mules.

Moorehouse and Daggett watched the buffalo hunters' wagon. "Whatta you think?" asked Daggett.

Moorehouse looked up and down the river. "A might swift for my likin', but if the rest hold the same line the buffalo hunters' took, and if they don't let the water scare 'em, there shouldn't be no problem. I'm sendin' 'em across."

Moorehouse stood at the river's bank and talked to each driver. 'Do what Dave Daggett tells you and you'll make it fine. Now, if you do happen to get into some kinda trouble, don't panic. There'll be men on horseback standin' by to give you a hand. I'll see you on the other side." Something he would repeat more than forty times that day.

Moorehouse sent the first three wagons across without the women aboard. After they crossed with no problem the women stayed with the wagons. He stood on the bank and nervously watched the crossing. After each successful crossing, Moorehouse would breathe a sigh of relief. He was satisfied and relieved the way things were going. One wagon had trouble when the oxen pulling it tried to turn downstream, but the riders stationed along the way roped the animals and pulled them back on course. A few wagons later, disaster struck. With no warning, the Ortman's oxen gave way to the current and lunged downstream. The downstream front wheel climbed a boulder and tilted the wagon back into the on-rushing water. It happened in the swiftest part of the river. The upstream side of the wagon was submerged. Water cascaded over the front of the wagon. Frank Ortman dropped the reins and grabbed his younger daughter Sarah who sat next to him. Charlotte gripped the seat with one hand and the side of the wagon with the other. Slowly her grip loosened and she was washed from the seat. Her father grabbed at her, catching the top of her blouse. It tore off in his hand and she was gone.

Red Eagle stood with Roth and Ledbetter on the far bank watching the crossing. When Charlotte was washed from the wagon, Red Eagle turned and sprinted down stream. Ledbetter dove into the river, but before he could reach the girl, she had swept past him.

Red Eagle ran along the bank looking back at Charlotte, her arms flailing in the water. He dove in and swam to intercept her, but she was going to pass him by. He turned downstream and with powerful strokes swam parallel to Charlotte, then worked his way over to her and grabbed her around the waist. Holding her with one arm and paddling with the other, he headed diagonally for the riverbank. She was frightened and clung tightly to him. When they were out of the current and in shallow water, he took her in his arms and carried her to the bank.

They sat quietly, catching their breath. Charlotte leaned against Red Eagle. He put his arm around her and said, "Pretty hair."

Charlotte stared at him, and started to laugh. Suddenly she realized she was naked from the waist up and jerked away, covering herself with both arms. Red Eagle took off his shirt and draped it around her.

A few minutes later they heard horse hooves. Luke Norton rode up. "Thank God you made it. Are you two all right," he asked.

"Yes," answered, Charlotte, pulling Red Eagle's shirt tight around her.

Luke dismounted and helped her onto the horse. Red Eagle followed along behind.

When the Ortman wagon had its trouble, men on horseback roped the wagon and held it steady while others lassoed the oxen and pulled them forward. It had been a close call, but the wagon made it across with Ortman and his younger daughter. However, everything in the wagon was soaking wet.

When Red Eagle and Charlotte arrived back at the crossing, Ortman left Sarah with Ellie, and ran to meet them. He pulled Charlotte from the horse and held her close. "Are you all right, honey?" he asked.

"I'm fine Papa. Where is Sarah?"

"She's with Mrs. Addison. She's okay." Ortman looked at the shirt Charlotte had draped around her. He pushed her away and took off his coat. "Here," he said, handing her the coat, "go behind the horse and get that shirt off. Now."

Charlotte did as she was told. Then walked over to Red Eagle, handed him his shirt and said, "Thank you."

Red Eagle took the shirt and nodded his head.

Moorehouse showed up with Ellie and Sarah. He smiled at Charlotte. "Welcome back," he said. "You gave us all a pretty good scare."

Sarah ran to Charlotte and hung onto her. "Oh, Charlotte, I was so scared."

Charlotte turned to Red Eagle. "He saved my life."

"Come on," said Frank Ortman, taking Charlotte by the arm. "We've got a lot to do." She jerked free. "But Papa, he saved my life." It was clear that Charlotte expected her father to acknowledge Red Eagle.

Ortman stared at the Indian. "Obliged," he said, then walked away. The girls followed.

"Well," said Moorehouse," pushing his hat back on his head, "that was one helluva thank you."

"A pretty big one coming from that man," said Ellie. "Maybe what happened to the ortmams today wasn't all bad."

CHAPTER EIGHT

Ledbetter took a burning twig from the fire and lit his pipe. Then spoke to Red Eagle in the tongue of the Cheyenne. "When we get to Fort Laramie tomorrow me and my partner'll get us a couple of mules and be on our way. You're welcome to come along if you want to."

Red Eagle's heart was saddened. He liked this strange one who spoke his tongue. He was also afraid. Ledbetter was the only friend he had. "You no want see faraway place?" he asked.

Ledbetter grinned. "No, this is as faraway from home as I wanna be."

"You go they make me go to?"

"They might. I've given that some thought. Come on, I want to talk to the medicine woman."

Ellie watched Ledbetter and Red Eagle coming her way and guessed what Ledbetter was going to ask. He was a disheveled looking little man with his soiled clothes and stringy blonde hair, but she felt underneath it all he was a decent person.

Ledbetter tipped his hat. "Evenin' Ma'am."

Red Eagle had no hat but went through the motions and echoed, "Evenin' ma'am."

Ellie smiled at the two of them. "What can I do for you Mr, Ledbetter?"

"Shore has been a purty day, ain't it?" Ledbetter said.

"Was there something you wanted Mr. Ledbetter?" asked Ellie.

Ledbetter turned and looked about. "Yesiree this has been a purty day, sunshine along with a good breeze."

"Yes it was a pretty day Mr. Ledbetter. Now is there something you want to talk to me about?"

Ledbetter took off his hat. "Well, Ma'am, me and my partner'll be strikin' out tomorrow."

"I figured as much," said Ellie, waiting for him to continue. Finally she said, "You want me to look after Red Eagle, right?"

Ledbetter looked at Red Eagle and back at Ellie. "I offered to take him with me, but he's hell bent on seein' that faraway place you folks are headin' fer. So I thought maybe you'd know someone that might could use some help. He's a good worker."

"I'm sure he is," said Ellie.

"That way," said Ledbetter, "might be Andy Moorehouse wouldn't run him off."

Ellie smiled. "Well now, Mister Ledbetter, it just so happens I could use some help. Someone to look after the animals and wagon while I look after my patients."

Ledbetter's face lit up. "That shore takes a load off my mind, ma'am. I don't know if I could've left him out here on his own."

Ellie said, "When you leave tomorrow, have him bring what belongings he has to my wagon."

"Thank you, Ma'am," said Ledbetter, as he turned to leave.

OUTSIDERS

"Just a minute, Mister Ledbetter," said Ellie. "I heard some folks talking about us leaving the Platte River. Does that mean water's going to be in short supply?"

"No Ma'am. You'll be followin' the Sweetwater. It goes all the way to South Pass."

"And after South Pass?"

"I don't rightly know, Ma'am. I ain't never been that far." Ledbetter shoved his hands deep into his pockets. "Ma'am, I don't know if Andy Moorehouse told you, but if I was you I'd get just enough supplies here at Fort Laramie to last to Fort Bridger. I've heard me some tall tales 'bout South Pass. Some say it's hard to cross over and some say it's not. I don't know, but no need loadin' your wagon down if you don't have to. Best be on the safe side."

"Wel,l thank you, Mr. Ledbetter, that's very thoughtful of you, but Andy already spoke to me about it." Ellie waited for Ledbetter to say something, but he just stood there. "Well Mr. Ledbetter, good luck to you and your friend."

"And to you too Ma'am," he said and walked away.

"Miister Ledbetter," Ellie called out.

He turned around. "Yes ma'am?"

"You're a good man."

Ledbetter smiled. "And you're a good woman."

The next day excitement ran heavy as the wagon train neared Fort Laramie. For the first time in weeks the travelers would get a hot bath, put on clean clothes and maybe sit at a table enjoying a meal prepared by others. Or just enjoy walking around, away from the wagons for a day. Women would replenish their supplies of flour and other foodstuffs and hope there was a place where they could buy needles, thread and fabric. Men would visit the blacksmith, make repairs on their wagons, exchange broken-down livestock for healthy animals and look for a place where they might get something to drink.

The people's excitement kindled Red Eagle's curiosity. "Place we stop. What like?"

"Not much," said Ledbetter. It's just a place where people trade for stuff they need. You wouldn't like it."

"Why I no like?" he asked.

"Because," Ledbetter hesitated, "You don't have anything to trade. Besides, you're not old enough so you stay with the wagons."

"You have be old for trade?"

Ledbetter blew up. "Dammit, these people ain't like other folks. There's too many of 'em, and they don't cotton to strangers, especially to Ind…Just you do like I say and stay with the wagons."

When Laramie came into sight just across the river, Red Eagle stared in awe. It was a shabby looking place with run down buildings. But it was his first look at real wooden structures, and to him they were something grand. He wanted to see all of them up close.

After Ledbetter and Roth left to search for a team of mules, Red Eagle took his belongings to Ellie's wagon. She wasn't there, so he threw them into the back and climbed up front where he sat and watched the people heading for the Fort. Then he spotted Charlotte; she was with her sister and her father. Red Eagle wondered why they could go to the Fort while he had to stay with the wagons. After all he was older and besides that, they were girls. He climbed down from the wagon and followed. The river was shallow, and they waded across.

Red Eagle stood inside the Fort and stared at all the people, especially the women in their colored dresses. He studied the wooden paths that ran along the front of some of the buildings, and strolled along, taking everything in. After an hour of sightseeing, Red Eagle decided to go back to the wagons. Just outside the Fort he saw two men standing in front of a building. They were laughing and talking. One was tall; the other was a little man, much shorter than Red Eagle. Suddenly the tall one jerked off his hat and began laughing and hitting the other man with it. Red Eagle could hear laughter and yelling inside the building. When the two men saw Red Eagle they grew quiet. He started around them, but they blocked his path.

"Are you in my way, Injun?" the tall one asked.

Remembering what Ledbetter had told him about the people here, Red Eagle turned away.

The tall one grabbed Red Eagle's shoulder and jerked him around. "He ain't very friendly, is he, Shorty? I asked you a question, Injun."

Red Eagle was angry. Why was this man whom he didn't know threatening him? Should he fight him? What would Ernie Ledbetter do? Again Red Eagle tried to walk around them, and again they blocked his way. Then the short one spoke up, "If you want by, then walk out in the street. Now, get movin'."

"No, you get movin," came a voice behind Shorty. It was Dave Daggett.

The two men turned to face him. "You aimin' to move us?" asked the tall one. His grin exposed chipped, yellow teeth.

Just then, Moorehouse, Roth and Ledbetter stepped out of the doorway behind Daggett. "You gotta problem, Dave?" asked Moorehouse.

"Nope."

"How 'bout you?" asked Moorehouse, nodding at the two men. "You fellows got a problem?"

"We ain't got no problem," said Shorty.

Roth spoke up, "Then maybe you two fellers better move on along before you do."

The two men stomped off. "Damned Injun lovers," muttered Shorty.

Ledbetter took Red Eagle by the arm and pulled him aside. "I told you to stay with the wagons."

"Why I stay wagon? All people here."

"Go on back to the wagons. I'll be along directly. Now go!"

Red Eagle didn't like being treated like a child, but he walked away.

CHAPTER NINE

Red Eagle watched Roth and Ledbetter hitch their mules to the wagon.

Ledbetter stopped what he was doing and walked over to him. "You listen, and listen good. Let what happened at the Fort today be a lesson to you. White people are not like your people. Don't trust 'em, If…"

"But you white," interrupted Red Eagle.

"That's true, but I'm married to an Indian, I live like an Indian, I think like an Indian." Then he said more to himself than to Red Eagle, "Hell, I am an Indian."

"What 'bout Jeff friend?" said Red Eagle. "You trust?"

Ledbetter grinned, "I've known Jeff for more than twenty years. That's longer than you've been alive. Hell yes I trust him."

A frown crossed Red Eagle's face. "He help me today, and so Dave Daggett, and Moorehouse, he help."

Ledbetter put his hand on Red Eagle's shoulder. "Sure they

helped you, but not because they like you. They helped you because they didn't like those other two yahoos."

"What 'bout medicine woman?" asked Red Eagle. "Not trust her?"

"The medicine woman you can trust. She's a good woman. Trust her, but no one else. One thing more, stay away from them two girls with the yeller hair. Their Daddy's full of hate."

"Let's go," shouted Roth, "we're wastin' daylight."

"We no see each other more?" asked Red Eagle.

"No," said Ledbetter, "we won't." He swung upon the wagon where Roth sat waiting. As they pulled away, Ledbetter leaned around the side of the wagon and yelled, "Go home."

Red Eagle stood motionless, staring after the wagon until it was out of sight.

While Red Eagle watched the wagon, Ellie watched Red Eagle. She felt a deep sadness for him. He was losing the only friend he had.

Ellie was surprised at how much English Red Eagle had learned in such a short time. Ledbetter had taught him well.

Every evening, Ellie made her rounds, treating the complaints of her patients, dispensing medicine and giving medical advice. Afterward, she would help Red Eagle with his English. One evening he asked, "What name of faraway place we go?"

"Its called California."

"Why go there?"

"Good question," said Ellie. "Some to start a new life, some to leave an old life, others, like yourself, for adventure."

"What mean word, add-venchure?"

Ellie thought for a minute. "How can I explain it?" Then, smiling at Red Eagle, she said, "To see what's on the other side of the mountain."

"I understand," he said. "What is like on other side of mountain?"

"I only know what I've read or heard. It has land like here," she said moving her arms in a sweeping motion, "only it's like summer all year. It has mountains, and places called deserts where it's so hot and dry, nothing can grow. Then there are the cities, with buildings two and more stories high, some right next to the ocean."

Red Eagle looked puzzled.

"The ocean," she said, "is a large body of water, a lake so big you can't see across it." She spread her arms, "Much wider than the distance you have traveled from your home."

Red Eagle didn't believe there was a lake that big, but decided if she believed it, then he wouldn't tell her that he didn't. Instead, he said, "If summer all time, how know what time year at?"

Ellie smiled, "We have something called a calendar. It shows what time of the year it is. I'll let you see it tomorrow, and explain it to you."

"You say building two stories, What stories?"

Ellie thought a minute. "It's houses stacked on top of each other."

"I want see California," Red Eagle said excitedly. "I want stay with wagon train."

"Then you have to make yourself essential."

"Make what?"

"Be needed," she said. Then smiled "Don't worry, I have a few ideas. I'll speak with Andy Moorehouse tomorrow."

"For Pete sake, Ellie," said Moorehouse, this is my livelihood, I can't let every tag-along that wants to go to

California ride for free. Hell, I shoulda left him at Fort Laramie. In fact I was goin' to, but after he had that run in with those two saddle tramps, I couldn't very well go off and leave him there."

"What happened?"

"It weren't much, just a couple of yahoos that had a little to much to drink, tryin' to be bigger then they were. It weren't the Indian's fault."

Ellie gave Moorehouse a big smile. "You know something, Andy Moorehouse? You're a hard man, but try as you may to hide it, now and then a little bit of compassion peeks through."

"Are you finished?" he asked.

"Just about," said Ellie, looking around. "Where's Dave Daggett?"

"He'll be along soon." Then Moorehouse gave her an uneasy look. "Whatta you wantin' to know for?"

"Oh, I was thinking about him riding around out there all by himself. Scouting must be an awfully lonely job. No one to talk to. No one to…"

"Stop it, Ellie. I know where you're headin'."

"Andy, use your head. We're in Indian country, and surprisingly, Red Eagle speaks pretty good English. If the need arose, Dave would have an interpreter. I think it would behoove you to give it some serious thought."

"You know something, Ellie, a lot of behoovin's been comin' my way lately, most of it from you. Anyway, you can forget it; Dave's a loner. He'd never go for it."

"I swear, Andy Moorehouse, sometimes I don't understand you at all. In fact, I don't think you understand yourself."

"What in the world are you talkin' about?"

"Really, Andy, you're the wagon master. Dave works for you, not the other way around."

"Now, Ellie, just you take it easy a minute. You don't have no idea how hard it is to find a seasoned scout you can count on. Dave Daggett's one of the bes…"

"Andy," Ellie broke in, "what's it going to be? You going to talk to him, or am I?"

As was his habit when trying to make a decision, Moorehouse took off his hat and wiped the sweatband with his neckerchief. "Awright, Ellie, I'll talk to Dave, I'll ask him if he wants to do what you want, but I ain't gonna order him to."

"Fair enough," said Ellie. "Just make sure Dave understands the benefits of having an interpreter with him. That's all I'm asking. If you can't explain it to him properly, then I will." Ellie walked away, leaving Moorehouse shaking his head.

"She wants what?" Daggett shouted.

"Ellie figures you need an interpreter," said Moorehouse.

"Well, she figured wrong."

"Look, Dave, you might oughta give it some thought. Could be it'd work out."

"Andy, you satisfied with the job I'm doin'?"

Moorehouse knew Dave's mind was made up, and there was nothing he could do to change it.

"Well?" said Daggett, waiting for an answer.

Moorehouse started laughing.

"What's so damned funny?"

"Now, Dave, you know I'm more'an satisfied with your scoutin', but Ellie feels sorry for you."

Daggett frowned at Moorehouse. "What the hell are you talkin' about?"

"Well now, let me see if I can remember just how she put it." Then, Moorehouse said in a high squeaky voice, "I feel so sorry for Dave, ridin' around out there all by himself, all alone, no one to talk to." Moorehouse could hardly finish for laughing.

Daggett swung up on his horse and looked down at Moorehouse. "You wanna hear somethin' funny, Andy? I think you and Ellie oughta get hitched and adopt that Indian." He spurred his horse away.

Red Eagle was now wearing white man's clothing. Ellie had asked some of the ladies if they would be willing to give her clothing in exchange for medical care. Mrs. Josie Mattingly, upon hearing the request, offered her son's entire wardrobe. Two months before her family started the trip west, her son, Edgar, passed away with yellow fever. But she had been unable to part with any of his belongings, and had hung onto everything, his clothes, hat, boots, pocketknife and books. Her husband told her, "Josie, it's time to let go." So with a heavy heart, she gave them up.

Red Eagle also had a haircut. Against his protests, Ellie had convinced him to let her cut his hair. After much discussion, a compromise was reached, she left it longer than the other men's hair.

The next day, dressed in his new clothes, Red Eagle unhitched the mules and led them to pasture. On his way back he met Charlotte and her sister. When Charlotte saw Red Eagle approaching, wearing his new clothes and sporting his new haircut, she took Sarah's arm and stopped her. "Look at Red Eagle," she said. "He's actually handsome."

"Charlotte," Sarah whispered, "you oughta be ashamed. What if someone heard you?"

Remembering what Ledbetter had told him about staying away from the two girls, Red Eagle kept his head down and passed them by.

When he didn't look up or speak, Charlotte called out, "Red Eagle, wait a minute, I want to talk to you."

He turned and stared at her. "I can no talk you," he said.

"Why? Did my Papa tell you not to?"

"No, friend Ledbetter."

"Oh him. Why'd he tell you something like that?"

"He say your father full of hate."

"You take that back," cried Sarah, running up to him with clinched fists. Red Eagle grabbed her by the arms and held her off.

"Sarah," shouted Charlotte. She caught Sarah around the waist and pulled her away.

Red Eagle turned and hurried back to Ellie's wagon. He didn't understand why the girl got so angry with him. He only told them what Ledbetter had told him. He decided to find Ellie and tell her what happened. She would know if he had done something wrong.

He had circled about a quarter of the wagons, when he spotted Ellie at Moorehouse's wagon. She was talking with Moorehouse and Dave Daggett.

As Red Eagle walked up to them, he heard Dave Daggett say, "Darn it, Ellie, I don't need…" He stopped talking when he saw Red Eagle.

Red Eagle blurted out excitedly to Ellie, "I tell something what happened, and you tell what I did."

Ellie stared at him. "What in the world are you talking about?" she asked.

"I say what Ledbetter say. They mad," said Red Eagle.

"What? Oh, never mind, We'll talk on the way back to the wagon." Then, she turned back to Moorehouse and Daggett. "You two are as stubborn as the mules that pull these wagons.

Come on Red Eagle." They started to leave, when some one shouted, "Wait just a minute, I want to talk to all of you." It was Frank Ortman.

Ortman walked up to Moorehouse. Pointing at Red Eagle, he said, "I want this Indian kicked off this train right now. If you don't do it, I will."

"Now, hold on just a minute," said Moorehouse, you ain't kickin' nobody off this here train."

"Then, you'd better do it yourself," shouted Ortman.

"Calm down," said Moorehouse, "and tell me why I'd wanna do somethin' like that."

"This Goddamned Indian savage manhandled my little girl, that's why."

Moorehouse glanced at Ellie and back to Ortman. "Watch your mouth," he said. Now, tell me what happened."

Ortman glared at Red Eagle. "He told my girls that I'm a hateful person. Then, shoved my youngest around."

Ellie broke in. "Red Eagle," she asked, "is this what you wanted to talk to me about?"

"Yes."

"What Mr. Ortman said, is it true? Is that what happened?"

"Yes."

"See," screamed Ortman, "He don't even deny it."

Ellie turned on Ortman. "Be quiet, Mr. Ortman. Now, Red Eagle, tell exactly what happened."

"They want talk. I say Ledbetter say I no talk them. He say father full of hate."

"Did you put your hands on the little girl?" asked Moorehouse."

"I held arms. She much angry."

Ellie turned to Ortman. "Tell me, Mr. Ortman," she asked,

"would you be this upset if Red Eagle wasn't an Indian?"

Ortman ignored the question and turned to Moorehouse. "He shouldn't be on this train, anyhow."

"Why?" asked Moorehouse, "because he's an Indian?"

"Because he's not paying his way like the rest of us. How come he's riding free?"

Before Moorehouse could answer, Daggett broke in. "He ain't ridin' free. He's my interpreter."

"Your interpreter?" yelled Ortman. "Since when?"

"Since yesterday," Daggett yelled back. Then glancing at Ellie, he said, "I decided I needed some company. Scoutin's a lonely job."

Ellie raised her eyebrows and smiled.

"Just you make sure he stays away from my girls," said Ortman, and stomped off.

Ellie watched him leave and said, "Now there goes a man without purpose." Then turned to Daggett and said, "Thanks, Dave."

"You know somethin', Ellie?" said Daggett. "If it was anyone but Frank Ortman, I'd swear you set this whole thing up." Then he turned to Moorehouse. "I thought you said you were gonna put that guy off this train at Fort Laramie?"

"Dammit, Dave, I couldn't kick him off without kickin' his two girls off too."

"Careful, Andy Moorehouse," said Ellie, "a little compassion's peeking through." Then she turned to Daggett. "Thanks again, Dave. You won't regret it."

"I already do," he answered.

CHAPTER TEN

Red Eagle sat straight and proud on the horse along with an old saddle that Andy Moorehouse had furnished him, He felt good riding alongside Dave Daggett. They left the wagon train at first light and had been riding almost two hours. Distant silvery clouds slowly turned pink as early morning sunrays illuminated them. The tops of the clouds billowed out like stalks of cauliflower. A gusty warm wind blew out of the southwest.

Through a sea of prairie grass, scattered with trees and shrubs the two men rode. Neither one had spoken since they left. Red Eagle broke the silence. "Where we go, Dave Daggett?"

Daggett reined his horse to a stop. "Look," he said, "the only reason you're out here is because I don't like that fellow, Frank Ortman. I shoulda kept my mouth shut back there and let Andy handle it. But that Ortman just rubs me the wrong way."

"He rub you?"

Daggett glared at Red Eagle. "Look, now that I'm stuck with you, there's a few things you better know. First, I'm used to workin' alone, so don't expect me to be battin' the breeze with you, and don't eve…"

"Battin' breeze?" Interrupted Red Eagle. "I no understand."

"That's what I'm talkin' about. Always askin' questions."

"I sorry, Dave Daggett. Where we go?"

Daggett started to say something, but shook his head. "We're gonna check out an arroyo up ahead. We're gonna see if it's dry, If so we'll pick up a trail along the North Platte River. It'll take us a little north to the Sweetwater."

"What Sweetwater is?" asked Red Eagle.

Daggett stared at Red Eagle. "You don't know a damned thing do you? Well, it's a windin' mountain stream that we'll follow west all the way to South Pass." Daggett spurred his horse on.

Red Eagle caught up with him. "You here before?" he asked.

"If you mean have I traveled through this country before, yeah. But I don't always remember every landmark, that's why I have to scout ahead of the train. That, and make sure there's no trouble up ahead."

"What trouble?"

"What kind of trouble? You oughta remember the river we had to ford. Then, there's always a chance we might run into some bad hombres."

"Bad Hombres?"

"Yeah, like those two buffalo hunters we picked up."

Red Eagle reined his horse to a stop. "They not bad hombres. Ledbetter my friend."

"Dammit, I'm not sayin' they were bad, but they could've been. You have to be careful out here. Don't trust anyone."

"That what friend Ledbetter say. He say no trust white man."

Daggett looked over at Red Eagle. "That's good advice. Did he tell you not to trust Indians?"

"No."

"He should've."

"But I..."

"Look, Red Eagle," Daggett cut in, "out here you don't trust anyone, red or white. Now, let's leave it at that."

Neither of them spoke the rest of the way to the arroyo.

Daggett dismounted and rolled a cigarette. Looking across the dry gully, he said, "It don't look like much now, but when there's a hard rain northeast of here, they ain't nothin' can cross. So full of water you just have to wait it out."

They crossed the arroyo and rode northwest about a quarter of a mile, then turned due west. In the distance the land became more wooded as it sloped upward toward the foothills.

Suddenly, Daggett reached over and grabbed Red Eagle's horse by the reins and stood up in his stirrups. He stared off in the distance. "I think we're gonna have company."

Red Eagle trained his eyes where Daggett was looking and could make out a group of riders along the tree line. "Who they?" he asked.

"My guess would be Indians," said Daggett.

"Good," said Red Eagle.

Daggett glared at Red Eagle. "Good? Whatta you mean good?"

"I afraid they be bad hombres."

Daggett shook his head. "Whites don't have a lock on bein' bad. You may learn that today."

"What we do?" asked Red Eagle.

"Well, said Daggett, "if we can see them, then they can see us. We're gonna ride back to the arroyo, put it between them and us. Then, we'll wait and see what happens. But ride slow, we don't want 'em to think we're in a hurry." When they were back across the arroyo, Daggett dismounted and dug an extra pistol out of his saddlebags. "You know how to use one of these?" he asked Red Eagle.

"No"

"You mean your *friend, Ledbetter*, didn't teach you? Too bad. But I guess it don't matter. Those Indians won't know that you don't know shit about a gun." He handed Red Eagle the pistol. "Here, stick it in your waistband."

Daggett reached down and pulled his rifle from its scabbard, and laid it across his saddle.

The two waited on the bank of the arroyo. Red Eagle looked over at Daggett. Then, reached down and fingered the butt of the pistol. He felt proud.

Seven Indian braves rode up and stopped on the opposite bank. Daggett was relieved to see they only had one rifle. The one with the weapon yelled something across at them.

Without taking his eyes off the Indian, Daggett asked, "What'd he say?"

"He want know why we do here."

"It's none of his damned business," said Daggett, then quickly added, "Don't tell him that. Tell him we're waitin' for a wagon train that's close behind us."

Red Eagle looked at Daggett. "But that no true. Wagon…"

"Dammit, Red Eagle, tell him what I told you to tell him."

Red Eagle relayed the message as he was told. Then, added, "We are passing through to a faraway place."

"Do you know of a man called Samuel?" asked the Indian.

"No."

"What is the man you are with called?"

"His name Dave Daggett."

"Just a damned minute," said Daggett, hearing his name called out. "Whatta you two talkin' about?"

"He look for man called Samuel. He want know your name."

"Let's get one thing straight right now," said Daggett. "You don't answer him 'til you check with me first. You tell me exactly what he says, and you tell him exactly what I tell you to say. Don't add anything. You understand?"

"I understand, Dave Daggett."

The Indian yelled something. Red Eagle turned to Daggett. "He say they come over. They want talk."

Daggett cocked his rifle. "Tell him he can come across, and bring the rifle with him. The rest are to stay where they are."

Red Eagle yelled the instructions across the arroyo.

The Indians argued. Then the one with the rifle started across.

Daggett reined his horse around where the rifle across his lap was trained on the Indian.

The Indian rode up next to Red Eagle, stared at him and asked, "What is your name?"

"I am Red Eagle, son of Gray Wolf."

"I am called Big Thunder," said the Indian. Then, he reached over and jerked Red Eagle's hat off. "Your hair and clothing tell me you have taken up the way of the white man."

Red Eagle turned to Daggett. "He say his name Big Thunder. He say I take way white man. He no like my dress. He..."

Daggett broke in. "I figured as much."

Red Eagle had been shamed. He lowered his eyes. "I have no other clothes," he told the Indian.

Big Thunder handed back Red Eagle's hat. "Who cut your hair?"

"I did," Red Eagle lied.

"Okay," said Daggett, "enough chitchat. Ask him why he's huntin' this fellow Samuel."

Red Eagle relayed the question.

"Because," said Big Thunder, "this man hurt my sister."

Red Eagle turned to Daggett. "He say man hurt sister."

Looking at Big Thunder, Daggett said, "Tell him we don't take a likin' to men who hurt women. If we run across this man, Samuel, we'll turn him over to the white man's law, or to the Indians, whichever we see first."

Red Eagle relayed Daggett's message.

Big Thunder stared at Daggett. Then spoke to Red Eagle.

Red Eagle turned to Daggett. "He say, he have no use for white man law, he say he thank you maybe good man."

Daggett nodded at Big Thunder. The two stared at each other for a moment before Big Thunder jerked his horse around and rode back across the arroyo. The Indians turned and rode away.

"They not bad hombres," said Red Eagle.

"No, they weren't," said Daggett.

"What we do now?" asked Red Eagle.

"Wait for the wagons. When they show up, we're finished for today." While Red Eagle watched the Indians in the distance, Daggett watched him. *Maybe,* he thought, *this interpreter idea might not be a bad thing.* Of course, he'd never tell Ellie. "Give me the pistol," he said to Red Eagle.

Red Eagle pulled the pistol from his waistband and handed it over, "You teach me pistol?" he asked.

"Yeah, I think I'd better."

CHAPTER ELEVEN

Andy Moorehouse poured two cups of coffee. He handed one to Daggett, blew on his own, and said, "So, Red Eagle was a help today, huh?"

"Well," said Daggett, "I can usually get across to an Indian as to where I'm goin' and why I'm goin' there, but those Indians we ran into today weren't in the best of moods."

Moorehouse grinned. "Then, what your sayin' is Red Eagle was a help today?"

Daggett took a sip of coffee. "I suppose."

"You suppose? For cryin' out loud, Dave, if he helped out, say so."

"Okay, so he helped out. Now, let's drop it."

Smiling from ear to ear Moorehouse shoved his hat back and said, "You gotta be sure to tell Ellie. She'll be mighty pleased to hear you two are hittin' it off."

Daggett frowned at Moorehouse and took out his smoking tobacco.

Moorehouse asked, "Them Indians by any chance didn't tell you what this Samuel fellow looks like, did they?"

"No, why?"

"Well, it just so happens we picked up a rider this afternoon. He asked to tag along 'til we get to Fort Bridger. Says he has a brother-in-law he's supposed to meet there."

"Did he give you a name?"

"Yeah, Jordan, but I don't know if it's his first or last name."

"Sounds like a last name to me. You better find out."

"You wanna take a stroll around the wagons with me?" asked Moorehouse.

"Sure. You know where to find this guy?"

"Nope, but he won't be hard to spot."

"How so?"

"You'll know when you see him."

They had covered about a third of the way around the wagons when they came upon Luke Norton, Jake Vines and Emmett Jones, playing poker with a stranger. While they stood watching the game, Moorehouse looked over at Daggett and nodded his head.

Daggett studied the man. He had a slender build, black hair combed straight back, and a thin mustache. He wore black of pants and a black coat over a dark gray vest. Daggett leaned over to Moorehouse and whispered, "Looks like a damned undertaker."

When the poker hand was finished, Moorehouse said, "Jordan, I see you've met my other riders." Nodding at Daggett he said, "This here's my scout, Dave Daggett."

The stranger looked up at Daggett. "Glad to know you."

"Likewise," said Daggett. "I didn't catch your name."

"Jordan, Sam Jordan."

Norton began dealing another hand.

"Well I'll be damned," said Daggett, "I think I might've run into a friend of yours today."

Jordan gave Daggett a suspicious look. Studying his cards, he said, "I don't see how that's possible, beings the only friend I've got this side of the Mississippi is at Fort Bridger. Gotta be a mistake."

"You reckon?" said Daggett.

Jordan gave Daggett a sharp look. "That's what I said. A mistake."

"Well," said Daggett, we'll be in Big Thunder's territory for the next few days. When I run into him, and I'm sure I will, "I'll let him know you're not the Samuel he's lookin' for."

All the men looked at Daggett.

"Big Thunder? An Indian?" asked Luke Norton.

"Yep."

Jordan stood up. "Well, gentlemen, its been a long day. Thanks for the game." He picked up his money and walked over to a nearby wagon where he had his bedroll laid out underneath.

"What the hell was that all about?" asked Jake Vines.

"Yeah," chimed in Jones, You broke up the game, and I'm down thirty-five

cents."

"The way you play," said Moorehouse, "you oughta be glad the game broke up. C'mon, Dave, let's go."

When they were out of earshot of the card players, Moorehouse said, "Whatta you think?"

Daggett glanced over at Moorehouse. "He's the one."

"That's my thinkin' too."

"Whatta you gonna do about him?"

Moorehouse pulled off his hat and went through the

motions of wiping the sweatband. "I don't know. Maybe your little talk back there'll scare him off. I sure hope so. I don't like the thoughts of turnin' a man over to the Indians, even if he is a sonofabitch."

Moorehouse poured two more cups of coffee, and dumped what was left on the fire.

"Mind if I make a suggestion?" asked Daggett.

"Feel free. I could use one right now."

"Simple, first thing in the mornin', give the guy his walkin' papers."

"Leave him on his own out here?"

"You're damned right. He was on his own when you picked him up today, wasn't he?"

Moorehouse took a sip of coffee. "I guess you're right. I sure don't want no trouble with those Indians."

"You're damned right, I'm right. He's one man. You can't put this train at risk over one no good sonofabitch, and that's what he is."

"Okay, I'll talk to him first thing in the mornin'. You wanna be there when I do?"

"Yeah, I think I'd better be."

It was still dark when Moorehouse shook Daggett awake.

Daggett rubbed the sleep from his eyes. "What time is it?" he asked.

"Early, but I wanna talk to Jordan without a bunch of people millin' around."

"Good idea."

The two men walked along the wagons and were met by Red Eagle, carrying a long stick. He fell in with them and asked, "I am late, Dave Daggett?"

"No. And what the hell is that?" said Daggett pointing at the stick.

"No pistol. I make spear."

Moorehouse started laughing. "It sure as hell don't look like no spear I ever saw."

Red Eagle held the stick in the air. "It not finished."

"Looks more like a...Hell, I don't know what it looks like," said Daggett, shaking his head.

"Where we go today, Dave Daggett?"

"Right now we're gonna take care of some business. Then, we'll be on our way."

Red Eagle fell in behind the two men. When they arrived at the wagon where Jordan was sleeping, Moorehouse stuck his foot under the wagon and gave him a nudge.

Jordan rolled out from under the wagon with a pistol in his hand. Moorehouse took a backward step. "You can put that thing away," he said.

Jordan looked them over and jammed the pistol in his waistband. "You oughta be more careful roustin' a fellow out of a sound sleep. Whatta you want?"

"Somethin' been botherin' me," said Moorehouse, so maybe you can clear it up."

"Yeah, like what?"

"Well," continued Moorehouse, "I've never put much stock in coincidences, but, you show up here with the same name of a man some Indians are lookin' for. Now, wouldn't you say that's a pretty big coincidence?"

"So what? And who's the Injun?"

Daggett spoke up, "Who the Indian is ain't none of your goddamned business. And for someone, who's been befriended, you're carryin' an awful big chip on your shoulder, Mister."

Jordan glared at Daggett. His hands dropped to his sides. "Maybe you'd like to try knockin' it off, *Mister?*"

Daggett took a step forward, and Jordan jerked the pistol from his waistband. There was a swooshing sound as Red Eagle brought the would-be spear down hard across Jordan's wrist. The pistol flew from his hand. He screamed out in pain and grabbed his wrist. Daggett stepped in and struck Jordan a crushing blow with his fist, sending him sprawling to the ground. Moorehouse picked up the pistol. Jordan scrambled to his feet and staggered backwards into the wagon. "The sonofabitch broke my arm," he yelled.

"It should've been your head, you sorry bastard," said Daggett.

"You wanna tell us why those Indians are after you," asked Moorehouse.

"Go to hell."

"Well," said Moorehouse, "we can always ask Big Thunder."

"Dammit, my arm's killing me."

Moorehouse turned to Red Eagle. "Go get Ellie. Tell her what happened here."

Jordan leaned against the wagon wheel, glaring at Red Eagle. "You sonofabitch," he muttered.

Daggett walked over took Jordan buy the shirt collar and pushed him to the ground. "Now, sit there and shut up."

People began stirring, men hitching mules and oxen to the wagons, and women preparing breakfast. Children dashed about in the cool morning air, playing tag.

Luke Norton and Jake Vines came by to get their orders for the day from Moorehouse.

Luke looked at Jordan. "What the hell's goin' on?"

"Nothin' to worry about," said Moorehouse. "I'll fill you in later. Right now, I want you to go find Nate. Tell him I wanna see him right away."

Luke climbed on his horse, and rode off.

Ellie showed up with Red Eagle carrying her medical bag. She went straight to Jordan. "Let me take a look at that injured arm."

Jordan stared at her. "You a doctor?"

"More or less," said Ellie rolling up his sleeve. "Now, where did you get hit? Never mind, I see where." Ellie looked around. "Red Eagle, break off two pieces of that stick."

"This spear," said Red Eagle.

"And a mighty good spear it is," said Moorehouse. He took the stick from Red Eagle, broke off two pieces, smoothed the ends with a knife and handed them to Ellie. She took hold of Jordan's arm just below the elbow, gripped his wrist, with her other hand, and began a steady pull. Jordan gritted his teeth and moaned. She then placed the two sticks on each side of his arm and wrapped it tight.

"Well, said Ellie, "that's about all I can do. I'll check back with you later." She poured out a thimble of liquid, "Here, drink this down, It'll ease the pain some," she said and left.

"I hope to hell she knows what she's doin'," said Jordan.

"Oh, dry up." Moorehouse said.

Nate showed up. "You wanted to see me, Andy?"

"Yeah," said Moorehouse. "I want you to ride in the supply wagon with Giles for a couple of days."

"Aw Hell, Andy, why me?"

Moorehouse looked around the wagon train, and back at Williams. "Well, I guess I could ask Emmett to do it, 'course, then I'd have to get someone to take his place ridin' drag. He probably needs a break from eatin' all that dust anyway."

Moorehouse looked all around. "Let's see, who could I get?"

"Aw right Andy, I'll ride in the damned wagon, but why?"

"See that fellow sittin' over there? His name is Sam Jordan. I guess you could say he's my prisoner. He drew a gun on Dave and got his arm broke for his trouble. Make sure he stays in the wagon and out of sight. Can I depend on you, Nate?"

"Sure Andy, I'll keep a close eye on him."

"Thanks, I appreciate it. And Nate"

"Yeah?"

"He strikes me as one smooth character, so don't even talk to him."

"No need to," said Nate.

Moorehouse rode over to the Harris wagon. "Tiny, you'll be followin' the supply wagon, and I've got a fellow in it under guard. I'm not lookin' for him to cause any trouble, but thought you oughta know."

"What'd he do? And who's guardin' him?"

"He's just a trouble maker, not part of this train. Nate Williams is watchin' him."

"Awright, Andy, I'll keep a watch."

"Thanks, Tiny."

Moorehouse rode up to the supply wagon. Nate had just showed up with Jordan. Giles and Nate helped Jordan up in the wagon, where he sat on some feed sacks. Moorehouse took a seat up front, facing him.

"Jordan, we can do this the easy way or the hard way," said Moorehouse. "It's up to you. Don't cause any trouble, keep out of sight, and I don't tie you up."

"You expect me to lay back here in this hot wagon like one of these feed sacks?"

"Yes, I do. And I don't think that's such a bad idea, while

we're still in Big Thunder's territory, do you?"

Jordan looked up quickly at Moorehouse, then away. "What's your intentions?"

"Well, right now it's getting' you to Fort Bridger."

"Then what? "

"To tell the truth, Jordan, I don't know, but I know one thing, a lot's gonna depend how you behave between here and there."

CHAPTER TWELVE

From a hillside Daggett and Red Eagle looked back across the prairie, where tall grass rippled in the wind like waves on water. They had gotten a late start and hadn't lost sight of the wagon train.

As they rode along, Daggett looked over at Red Eagle. "I want you to listen and listen good. If we meet up with any Indians today, don't say anything about the man you hit with your club, and…"

"Not club. Spear."

Daggett glared at Red Eagle. "And you don't volunteer anything."

"What volunteer?"

"Dammit, you tell 'em only what I tell you to tell 'em. You don't add anything. Do you understand?"

"I understand, Dave Daggett."

"Dammit, Red Eagle, quit callin' me Dave Daggett."

Red Eagle looked puzzled. "But that your name."

"That's both my names."

"I no understand."

"Look, Red Eagle, just call me Daggett, not Dave Daggett."

"You no like front name?"

Daggett shook his head. "Just call me Daggett, okay?"

Red Eagle looked confused, and said, "Call me Eagle."

"For Crissake, Red Eagle, your two names go togeth…" Daggett suddenly broke off the conversation and reined his horse to a stop. "Hold it," he said.

"I see too, Dave Daggett."

A small band of Indians were crossing in front of them, about a quarter of a mile up ahead.

Daggett looked back for the wagon train, It could barely be seen, wending its way across the prairie.

"What we do?" asked Red Eagle.

"We wait here and hope they keep goin'." He squinted his eyes and stared at the Indians. "Can you see if Big Thunder is with 'em?"

Red Eagle stood in his stirrups and shaded his eyes. "He is," said Red Eagle. "But he good hombre."

"He was yesterday, he may not be today. Oh shit," said Daggett.

The Indians turned and rode toward them.

Daggett looked over at Red Eagle. "Remember what I told you. Don't say anything about the stranger, and you tell them only what I tell you to. Do you understand?"

"Yes, Dave Daggett, I no volunteer anything."

Daggett jerked the rifle from its scabbard and laid it across his lap. Then he took the spare pistol from his saddlebags and handed it to Red Eagle. Red Eagle held the pistol in his hand, admiring it.

"Dammit," said Daggett, "stick it in your waistband."

As the Indians approached, Daggett was glad to see they still had only one rifle, and like yesterday, it was carried by Big Thunder.

Holding his hand in the air, Big Thunder halted the party and shouted a greeting. Daggett waited patiently while Big Thunder spoke. When he finished, Red Eagle said, "He say they search for one called Samuel, but no find him. He say they must two places see."

"And I wonder where that would be?" muttered Daggett.

Red Eagle started interpreting, and Daggett stopped him.

Big Thunder spoke again. When he finished, Red Eagle looked at Daggett. "He say, one called Samuel lies in bowels of earth, or walk among white man. He say this truth, because brother saw him in dream inside white..." Red Eagle stopped, frowned, and asked, "What is cover baby. Uh baby bug?"

Daggett thought a minute, then, said, "Cocoon. Now, ask him in what way did the man mistreat his sister?"

Red Eagle relayed the question.

Big Thunder spoke with anger. When he finished, Red Eagle said, "He say man dishonor sister in way he no talk white man."

"It ain't hard to figure out what happened," said Daggett, then quickly added, "Don't tell him that. Tell him I'm sorry for his troubles."

Big Thunder spoke, waving his arms. Then fell quiet.

Red Eagle said, "He much angry. He say he find one called Samuel in white cocoon."

"C'mon," said Daggett, jerking his horse around, "we have to get back to the wagons."

Daggett kept his horse at a slow walk. He didn't want Big Thunder to think he was in any hurry.

Red Eagle asked, "When Big Thunder say white cocoon, he mean wagon?"

"Yes."

"He think stranger Samuel in wagon?"

"That's right."

"He wrong."

Daggett looked at Red Eagle. He decided not to tell him the truth. Not yet.

When Daggett and Red Eagle approached the wagon train, Moorehouse rode out to meet them. "How come you're back? Please don't tell me there's a problem."

Daggett pushed his hat back. "Afraid so. But nothin' that can't be taken care of." He told Moorehouse about his conversation with Big Thunder.

"By God, that's it," said Moorehouse, jerking his horse around.

Daggett caught up with him. "What you aimin' to do?"

"I'm gonna run him off, that's what."

"That oughta take care of the problem."

"He say what I think he say?" asked Red Eagle.

Daggett looked around at Red Eagle. "Go to Miss Ellie's wagon. She may need you."

Red Eagle opened his mouth to say something. Then he rode off.

Moorehouse and Daggett rode up to the supply wagon and dismounted.

"What's goin' on?" asked Nate Williams. "Why'd we stop?"

"Get your prisoner outta the wagon," said Moorehouse. "Giles, you saddle his horse."

Both men knew by Moorehouse's tone of voice not to ask any more questions and do as they were told.

Jordan climbed down from the wagon and gave Moorehouse a hateful look.

Giles kept busy with the saddle.

"Help him on his horse," said Moorehouse.

"I don't need your damned help," snapped Jordan, jerking away from Nate Williams. He put his foot in the stirrup, grabbed the saddle horn with his good arm and heaved himself up into the saddle. He glared at Moorehouse. "If you think you're runnin' me off, think again. I didn't exactly enjoy your hospitality."

Moorehouse walked over and handed Jordan's pistol to him. "If I was you, I'd head back toward Fort Laramie, and I wouldn't let any grass grow under them horse hooves." With that, he gave the horse a hard slap on the rump.

Daggett stood next to Moorehouse, watching Jordan ride away. "I know he's a no-good sonofabitch," said Daggett, "but I can't help but feel a little sorry for him."

"Don't waste your pity on the likes of him," said Moorehouse. "His type has a an uncanny way of survivin'."

CHAPTER THIRTEEN

Daggett and Red Eagle rode along the northern slopes of rolling hills. The plains spread out behind them where tawny grass waved golden in the sun.

It had been four days since Jordan rode off, and they had seen no sign of Big Thunder and his band.

"Miss Ellie angry at Andy Moorehouse," said Red Eagle.

"Oh, how so?" asked Daggett.

"She say wrong send stranger away with broke arm."

"She said that, huh? Does she know why Andy run him off?"

"She no say."

"Do you know why?"

"He was bad hombre?"

"He was that," said Daggett. "Remember Big Thunder telling us about the man who mistreated his sister?"

Red Eagle looked over at Daggett. "Stranger Samuel?"

"Sure was."

"I see Big Thunder," said Red Eagle.

Daggett reined up, and shaded his eyes. "Where?"

"No here," said Red Eagle. "Near Wagons."

"When?"

"Night stranger left."

"Why in hell didn't you tell someone?"

"I no talk him."

"It don't matter if you talked to him or not. You should've told me you saw him. Which way was he headin'?"

"Way we come from."

"How many was with him?"

Red Eagle thought a minute. Then held up four fingers. "I not know I must tell you, Dave Daggett, I not know."

"Well," said Daggett, "no matter. They ain't much we could've or would've done anyway."

Later that day, Daggett and Red Eagle sat alongside the old wagon trail, eating cold beef and hardtack.

"You hear?" asked Red Eagle.

Daggett quit eating and listened. He heard the faint sound of horse hooves. "Mount up," he said. "We'll move up on the side of the hill."

Daggett pulled his rifle from its scabbard and handed the extra pistol to Red Eagle. He watched the trail and waited. Red Eagle held the pistol out admiring it. Daggett looked over at him. "Dammit, put that thing away or give it back. It's not a play purty."

Red Eagle took one more look at the pistol and stuck it in his waistband.

The riders had their horses at a walk. Three riders came into sight with Big Thunder in the lead. All three of them looked beat. Big Thunder looked up the hill at Daggett and Red Eagle. Daggett thumbed back the rifle hammer. Big Thunder didn't stop or speak, just stared at them as he slowly rode past. He was wearing a black coat.

"Well," said Daggett, "Looks like Jordan's survivin' skills run out." Then he saw a horse dragging a travois with two bodies. "Well," said Daggett, "Looks like Jordan didn't go down easy."

"Big Thunder wear stranger coat?" asked Red Eagle.

"Afraid so," said Daggett. "Give me the pistol."

Red Eagle pulled the pistol from his waistband. Daggett reached for it, but stopped. "Keep it," he said, "I reckon you've earned it."

Red Eagle's face lit up. Then he looked at the pistol and held it out to Daggett. "I no can keep."

Daggett stared at Red Eagle. "What the hell you mean, You no keep?"

"I no have nothing give you."

"Take the damned pistol," Daggett yelled. "Just you keep it outta sight back at the wagons. And whatever you do, make damned sure Ellie don't see it."

Suddenly, clouds hid the sun and darkened the sky. And there was a muttering of thunder. Ragged edges of dark clouds peeked over the hills.

"We'd better head back to the wagons," said Daggett. "Looks like we'll be settin' up camp early today."

"Wait," said Red Eagle. He dismounted and began tightening his saddle cinch. The horse sweledl up, and Red Eagle kneed the horse in the stomach. Suddenly, there was a blinding light followed by a deafening cracking sound. Red Eagle could see his blue shirt through closed eyes. When he opened his eyes and looked around, everything had a reddish tint. Daggett and the horses were gone. Then, he spotted Daggett, lying on the ground. His head was bleeding. Red Eagle ran over to him. "Wake up, Dave Daggett," he shouted.

Daggett moaned, and opened his eyes. "What happened?" he asked. Then looking around, he yelled "The horses, where's the horses?"

"I find," said Red Eagle.

"No, wait. Help me up."

When the lightning struck, the horses bolted and were standing in the tall grass on the prairie.

"Stay, I get horses," said Red Eagle.

"No," answered Daggett, "keep behind me, they're skittish. We don't wanna spook 'em any more'n they already are."

They walked slowly toward the horses, but when they came within a couple hundred feet, the horses turned and ran.

Daggett sat down. "I'm getting' a little woozy," he said. "Let me rest for just a minute."

Red Eagle kept walking toward the horses, but again, they ran away.

"Dammit, Red Eagle," Daggett yelled, "Wait 'til my head clears. You're gonna have them horses outta sight."

Red Eagle stopped, held his arms out sideward, palms up, and began softly chanting. The horses stopped, turned, and looked at Red Eagle. He stood stone still and kept up the chanting.

Daggett struggled his feet, but his head ached and he felt unsteady. He sat back down, and watched and waited. After about ten minutes, the horses started walking slowly back toward Red Eagle. Daggett looked in wonder as the horses walked up and stood on each side of Red Eagle, and began to nuzzle his hands. Red Eagle took them by their bridles, and led them back to where Daggett sat.

Daggett stared at Red Eagle with a look of amazement. "What the hell was that?" he asked.

"Horses scared, I say no fear."

Daggett looked around. The sky was clearing up, just a few drops of rain. "Looks like it's over," said Daggett, mounting his horse. "Just a thunder storm passin'."

"Look!" cried Red Eagle, pointing to the southwest.

A wall of smoke rose along the horizon. Daggett checked the wind direction, and kicked his horse into a gallop. "C'mon," he yelled at Red Eagle. "We've gotta warn the wagons."

Andy Moorehouse saw Daggett and Red Eagle riding hard, and rode out to meet them. "Somethin' wrong?" he asked. Then he saw the blood on Daggett's face. "What the hell happened to you?"

"Never mind me," said Daggett, "looks like we've got us a prairie fire to the southwest. We gotta get these wagons movin."

"Damned lightnin'," said Moorehouse. "Go find Luke, Jake and Emmett. Tell 'em to spread the word we're movin' out." As Daggett rode off, Moorehouse shouted, "You know what's south of here?"

"No," Daggett yelled back, "but we got no choice. South it is."

CHAPTER FOURTEEN

The wagon train was alive with activity. Men hurriedly hitched up animals to wagons. Women complained because their cooking was interrupted, saving what they could of the supper meal and putting everything else away. When all was done, the wagons started moving south.

Daggett and Red Eagle joined Moorehouse at the head of the column.

"I sure hope we don't run into anything that'll hold us up," said Moorehouse. "Maybe you'd better ride on ahead for a look see."

Daggett checked the smoke on the horizon. "If we can make eight, maybe ten miles with no problems, we oughta be outta its path."

Red Eagle broke in. "Why go that way?" he asked, pointing south.

"I don't know about that," said Moorehouse, ignoring Red Eagle. "But if we push hard, we maybe can make five or six miles before dark." Moorehouse gazed at the smoke. "Damned prairie fires anyhow. You'd better get goin'. If there's somethin' blockin' our way the sooner we know, the better."

"Why go that way?" Red Eagle asked again. Daggett looked at Red Eagle, then turned back to Moorehouse. "As long as there's nothin' ahead to stop us, I'll keep on ridin'. So as long as you don't see me, keep on comin'. If I run into any trouble I'll hightail it right back and let you know."

"Why go that way?" Red Eagle asked again, pointing south.

"Not now, Red Eagle," said Daggett.

"No!" Red Eagle shouted. "I want know now why go that way."

Moorehouse and Daggett exchanged glances, surprised at Red Eagle's outburst.

Daggett dismounted. "Get down here and be quick about it. I'll show you. Then I don't want anymore questions." Daggett took out his knife, and squatted down. "Look," he said, drawing an X in the dirt. "This is us. That's south in front of us, this is north behind us, over here, that's west, and here is east. Now the fire is to the southwest of us, comin' this way," he scratched a line in the dirt. "But it's movin' to the north too, which is good. We're gonna dodge it by goin' south and let it pass us to the west." Then he stood up. "Kinda get behind it. See?"

Red Eagle stared at Daggett, then squatted down and studied the lines in the dirt. "Say me again why we go that way?" he said, pointing south.

Moorehouse burst out laughing, and Daggett lost his temper. "Dammit go on back to Ellie's wagon. She wants you."

Red Eagle gave Daggett a puzzled look. "What?"

"Go on. Ellie's calling you. Now get."

Red Eagle frowned. "I no hear Miss Ellie."

"By God I do. Now go and see what she wants."

He glared at Daggett and walked away leading his horse.

Moorehouse grinned and started to say something, but Daggett cut him off. "I'm not in the mood, Andy."

Red Eagle turned and shouted, "I leave wagon train now."

"Is that a fact," said Daggett, "and just where are you gonna go to?"

"I go to Ireland," he yelled.

Daggett kept his horse at a steady lope, keeping a close watch on the smoke in the distance. It was still drifting more north than east, which was good, as long as there wasn't a change in the wind direction.

After a couple of miles he topped the crest of a rise and jerked his horse to a stop. "What the hell," he muttered. In the valley below were buffalo as far as he could see. He stared in wonder. Never had he seen anything like it. He checked the smoke again, and headed back to the wagons at a full gallop.

When Moorehouse saw Daggett, he rode out to meet him. "Trouble?" he asked, looking worried. Daggett told him about the buffalo.

"How far ahead of us would you say them buffalo are?" Moorehouse asked.

"I'd say 'bout two miles, maybe even closer."

"Well, shoot. Don't this beat all, gettin' caught between a herd of buffalo and a prairie fire. Which way were they headed?"

"They weren't movin', just millin' around."

Moorehouse shook his head. "I don't know a helluva lot about buffalo. You think if somethin' spooks 'em they might stampede like cattle do?"

Daggett shrugged. "Hell, your guess is as good as mine. I hope not."

Moorehouse studied the smoke. "Looks like we're out of the fire's path. I'm gonna move the wagons to that high ground over there to the east. I don't wanna get any closer to them buffalo than I have to."

"Andy, I think we'd better have an early call in the morning. If that herd of buffalo starts movin' north, we'll be camped here two, maybe three days waitin' for 'em to pass."

"That many, huh?"

"I swear, Andy, I've never seen anything like it. Buffalo as far as the eye could see."

"I'll take your word for it. How 'bout fillin' Luke and Jake in on what's takin' place, and tell Nate Williams I wanna see him."

"I'll do that, but tell me, Andy, whatta you think about meandering north-west in the mornin' 'til we pick up the main trail? It'd save a little time."

Moorehouse looked around at the wagons. "I don't think so, Dave. I don't know what that burned-out area looks like, but it must be pretty bad. What if for some reason or another, we'd get stuck out there? No, I'm headin' straight north back to the main trail and the river. At least we'll have water."

"You're probably right. But if it's all right with you I'd like to cheat west just a little."

"Okay, but don't strike out too far west. We don't know what the main trail looks like either. The fire had to burn all the way up to the river."

"Aw to hell with it. Probably a bad idea anyway. I'll see you in the morning."

A few minutes later Williams showed up. "What's happenin' Andy?"

"Seems we've got a helluva herd of buffalo up ahead. I want you to put on some extra guards tonight. Make sure they stay alert, and listen for anything unusual."

"Like what?"

Moorehouse gave Williams a disdainful look. "Like what? Like maybe a thunderin' herd of buffalo bearin' down on us. Gawddammit, what did I just tell you? Don't you ever listen?"

"Sorry, Andy, I...uh...I'll get right on it."

"Just a minute. Pass the word that everyone'd better save some of their supper for breakfast cause we'll be pullin' out extra early in the mornin', and there ain't gonna be no time for cookin'."

"Right away, Andy," said Williams, hurrying off.

Next morning before dawn, the wagon train was on the move, with much grumbling about having to eat cold leftovers from yesterday's supper, and no coffee.

Daggett had left earlier, taking a north and little west direction, deciding to angle back to the original trail. He traveled alone, having left Red Eagle with Ellie. The air was heavy with the smell of burnt grass. The storm had passed, taking the clouds with it, leaving the sky clear. When Daggett entered the burned area, he found a wasteland. No foliage, tree trunks scorched bare, their blackened twisted leafless limbs were a pitiful sight. No animals or bird sounds. A vast silence reigned over the land. His horse's hooves stirred up ash, sending black powdery dust into the air. "Christ," he said aloud. "This must be the way hell looks." He felt sorry for those back with the wagon train. It must be rough going with the wagons stirring up all the black soot.

Daggett turned straight north. Around eleven o'clock, he reached the westward trail at the Platte river. He and his horse were covered with black soot. Dismounting, he slapped the dust from his pants with his hat, dug out a coffeepot, and scrounged around for firewood.

As he sat watching the coffee perk, he pondered his future. Something he had given a lot of thought to lately. He was thirty-two years old, and having watched the families on the wagon train, he felt cheated. Should he quit his job and settle down? If so, he'd have to talk to Moorehouse, and soon. He hated the thought. Moorehouse was getting up in years and had never been married; if he had he'd never mentioned it. Maybe he never wanted to get married. Would he understand? Probably not.

Daggett was enjoying his second cup of coffee when he spotted a small, black dusty cloud to the east. He kept an eye on it. As the cloud drew closer, he could make out three wagons. Daggett stood away from the trail and waited. When the wagons approached, he saw a man and woman in the lead wagon. The people in the following wagons had kerchiefs covering their faces. When they pulled up, Daggett walked upwind until the dust settled.

"Howdy," called the man from the wagon. "You in some sort of trouble?"

"No, no trouble."

"Whatta you doin' way out here by yourself?"

"I'm scoutin' ahead of a wagon train."

"Oh, thank God," the woman said.

The man spoke up. "We've been chasin' your wagons all the way from Fort Laramie. We got in there several days after you left and have been tryin' to catch up with you ever since. I take it you got out of the prairie fire's path?"

"Yeah, we dodged it."

The man climbed down from the wagon and stuck out his hand. "Name's Seymour, Amos Seymour." Then motioning back to the wagon, he said, "and this here's my wife, Edna." She smiled at Daggett; he tipped his hat and said, "Nice to meet you Ma'am. My name's Dave Daggett."

"Daggett? said Mr. Seymour. "I knew of some Daggetts back in Missouri. That wouldn't be some of your people, would it?"

"Afraid not."

The men from the other two wagons walked up. They looked strange without the kerchiefs on. Above and below where their kerchiefs had been worn, their faces were black, making them look like they were wearing bandit masks. Daggett immediately thought of raccoons. Seymour introduced them as Earl Daws and Tom Reed. They shook hands around. Daws said, "You'll have to meet our wives later. They're determined to stay inside the wagons 'til we're out of this burnt area."

Seymour yelled back to his wagon, "Dorie, Come on out and get acquainted."

A voice from inside the wagon said, "I'm a mess, Daddy."

"We're all of us a mess, honey. Come on out and meet Mister Daggett. He's from the wagon train we've been chasing."

A girl looking to be in her late teens pulled back the canvas. Smoothing her hair with her hands, she took a seat next to her mother. Daggett stood staring at her. She was beautiful, black shiny hair and crystal blue eyes. Her face glowed from having been rubbed with a damp cloth.

"Mr. Daggett," said Seymour, "This here's my daughter, Dora Marie."

Daggett mumbled a greeting and touched the brim of his hat.

Seymour asked, "Whatta you think the wagon master'll charge us to tag along as far as Fort Bridger?"

"I don't know," said Daggett, still staring at Dorie. "He's a fair man." Then, he turned to Seymour. "You're not goin' to California?"

"Oregon," said Seymour. "Ain't that where the trail splits? At Fort Bridger?"

"There abouts," said Daggett

"Got any idea how much farther before we're outta this danged burned out area?" Tom Reed asked

"That's what I aim to find out," said Daggett. "Look, the wagon train oughta be showin' up here in about three maybe four hours, dependin' on how much trouble they're havin' with all this black dust. I've gotta ride on ahead, but you're welcome to my fire while you're waitin', unburned wood's a little scarce around here right now. And there's still coffee in the pot. Feel free to help yourself."

"That's mighty good of you Mr. Daggett," said Mrs. Seymour. "We appreciate it."

"Glad to help," said Daggett. He swung upon his horse, looked over at Dora and rode off. After a couple of miles, Daggett found less fire damage. Apparently, the wind out of the southwest had kept the fire from spreading too far westward. A mile farther and he was out of it. It was good to breathe fresh air, to be rid of the foul smell of burnt grass and scrub brush. Daggett felt sorry for those on the wagons, and what they must be enduring. He would have to ride back and catch the wagons before they circled up for the night. Nobody was going to complain about an extra hour of travel if it meant getting out of the burnt area.

CHAPTER FIFTEEN

Daggett stood next to the supply wagon eating supper, balancing his tin plate on the wagon wheel.

"Mr. Daggett."

He recognized Dora's voice, turned, and knocked his plate off the wheel.

"I'm sorry," she said. "Did I startle you?"

"No...no, miss" he stammered, bending down to retrieve his plate. When he straightened up, she handed him his coffeepot. "Here's your pot. Mama wanted me to thank you, and I wanted to thank you too."

"Tell Mrs. Seymour that's not necessary, Miss. I was glad to help."

"Just the same, it was awfully nice of you, Mister Daggett."

He looked at he and said, "Would you call me Dave? Miss, I'm not used to being called Mister."

She smiled at him, "Only if you quit calling me Miss."

They both laughed. "Should I call you Dora?"

"Everyone calls me Dorie."

"Dorie, that's a pretty name. And so is your middle name."

She frowned at him. "How do you know what my middle name is?"

"Your Dad called you Dora Marie."

"And you remembered?"

Daggett's face reddened. "Well…uh…yeah."

An awkward silence followed. Daggett moved a pebble around with the toe of his boot. Finally, Dorie spoke up. "I've got to get back to the wagon and help Mama with supper." Thanks again for the coffee."

As she turned to leave, Daggett said, "Mis…uh, Dorie, maybe I could show you around the wagons sometime, let you meet some of the folks."

Dorie stopped and turned around. "That would be nice. Maybe tomorrow?"

"Sure."

"Thank you Dave." She walked away looking back at him and stumbled on an exposed tree root. Daggett made a move to help her, but she smiled and waved him away.

Daggett stood watching her. When he turned to get his dish, there stood Moorehouse, grinning. "Pretty girl," he said,

"Just tryin' to be neighborly."

"Uh huh."

"Uh huh? Whatta you mean, uh huh?"

"C'mon, Dave, like I said, she's a pretty girl."

"Whatta you want, anyhow?"

"Whatta you mean, whatta I want? As soon as Luke, Jake and Emmett get here we're gonna go over tomorrow's workload like we always do." Grinning, Moorehouse said, "that is if you can get your head outta the clouds long enough."

"That's real funny, Andy. I don't know why we bother with these damned get-to-gethers anyway. We're gonna do tomorrow what we did today and yesterday, and the day before that, and the day before that. I do the scoutin', you take care of the wagons, and Luke and his bunch ride along lookin' pretty. Well, you can have your meetin' without me." Dave stomped off, leaving Moorehouse standing there, smiling.

Moorehouse's crew, minus Daggett, stood around the supply wagon swapping stories when Nate Williams showed up grumbling about the prairie fire's aftermath.

"Hell," said Jake Vines, "be glad you weren't caught in the fire."

"I'd just soon've been in the fire as in that damned black soot," said, Nate, slapping his pant legs with his hat.

"Oh, quit your damned whinin'," said Emmett Jones. "Try ridin' drag through all that burnt out mess, and then you'll have somethin' to complain about."

Andy Moorehouse came from around the back of the wagon. "All of you pipe down, and listen up. Barring any unforeseen calamity, we oughta be at South Pass in a couple a weeks. Luke, with the river on your side, move over and spend a little more time with Jake."

"Where's Dave?" asked Emmett.

"He's...uh...he's takin' care of some personal business."

"What kinda personal business?" asked Williams

Moorehouse glared at him. "Dammit, Nate, what the hell did I say? You know what personal means? I swear if......Oh, to hell with it. I don't know why we bother with these damned get togethers anyway. We're gonna do the same thing tomorrow that we did today and yesterday, and the day before that and the day before that. Now go on, get to hell outta here, all of you."

Early next morning, Daggett was saddling his horse when Red Eagle rode up. "Well, well," said Daggett, "If it ain't O'Red Eagle. I thought you went to Ireland?"

Red Eagle lowered his eyes. "Miss Ellie say I can no get there from here."

Daggett grinned. "Well, I'm sorry to hear that. But since you're still here, whatta you say let's ride out and see what's goin' on in this part of the world?"

"No funny, Dave Daggett."

The two of them rode along in silence; the river on their right, and wind-whipped grassland on their left. Daggett was thinking about Dorie, while Red Eagle was wondering if Daggett's silence meant he was still angry. He decided to speak up. "Andy Moorehouse say we soon at South Pass."

"Uh huh."

"Miss Ellie sick last night."

"Uh huh"

"You sick?"

Daggett came out of his thoughts. "What? Whatta you talkin' about?"

"You no talk, I think maybe you sick like Miss Ellie."

"Dammit, can't a man do a little thinkin' without somethin' being wrong?"

"What think about?"

Daggett looked over at Red Eagle. "What think about? I'm thinkin' I made a big mistake takin' you on."

"No mistake. I big help. Miss Ellie say so."

"Oh, she did, did she? And you believe everything she says?"

"She much wise woman."

"Yeah, sometimes too much."

"Where we go, Dave Daggett?"

"I don't know. Sometimes I wonder why I go at all."

"I no understand. I think maybe you sick. You crazy talk."

"Never mind, Red Eagle. I was just thinkin' about someone…I mean somethin'." Daggett spurred his horse on ahead.

Late in the afternoon, Daggett jerked his horse around. "C'mon, let's go back and meet the train. I don't feel like waitin' for 'em."

"Wait, Dave Daggett," said Red Eagle. He reached in his pocket and brought out a circular flat stone. "Here I give you this."

"Daggett held it up and looked at it. What the hell is it?"

"It flat. It give you uh-uh, what you call? It…bring…what you call, Dave Daggett?"

"It brings good luck?"

Red Eagle's face lit up. "Yes flat stone give you good luck. I give you for pistol. You like?"

Daggett started to say something, but when he looked at Red Eagle and saw how pleased he was, he stuck it in his shirt pocket. Thank you Red Eagle, I'll always keep it with me." Daggett dismounted. "We'll wait here for the wagons."

Dorie handed Daggett a jelly biscuit sandwich, smiled and said, "Dessert?"

Dave took the sandwich, and gazed out over the river. "You know, I've been through here before, but this is the first time I've enjoyed it. Nice company, nice picnic," then he held up the jelly sandwich, "and a great dessert."

Dorie laughed. "You're easy to please. You know what Dave? It's good to have a day off the trail. To do what you want to do for a whole day. I should be ashamed, but I'm glad those two wagons broke down." Then she turned and faced him. "Dave, the other night I saw you reading a book. Would you lend it to me? That is when you finish it."

"A book? Oh, you mean the dairy."

Dorie looked flustered. "I'm sorry, Dave. I didn't know it was your diary."

"It's not my diary."

"Okay, your journal," she said, and smiled. "Women call them diaries, and you men call them journals."

"It's a dairy," he said, "but not mine. I took it off off a grave my last trip."

"Dave! Why would you do that?"

"It was wrapped in oil cloth, but the animals had chewed it up pretty good. I took it to save it. I don't know why. I know it sounds dumb, but someone had done a lot of writin' in it, and I just couldn't leave it there."

Dorie frowned. "But you were reading it."

"C'mon, Dorie. I wasn't intendin' to be nosey. I started readin' it to see who it belonged to." Dave reached over and took her by the arm. "Look, Dorie, there's nothin' personal in it. Like you said, it's a journal, a record of their trip. About the troubles they had along the way. About their animals, about the Indians they ran into, the trouble they had with their wagons a list of spare parts and other things they shoulda brought along. I've learned a lot from it." Daggett reached over and took her hand. "Look Dorie, the more we know what problems the ones who went before us had, the more we know what to look-out for. What to expect. God, Dorie, I don't want to scare you, but you know what people call the Oregon Trail?"

"No, what"?

"The longest graveyard in the country. C'mon Dorie,

weren't you a little scared before you joined this wagon train?"

"Just once, but it didn't amount to anything. In fact it turned out funny."

"What happened?"

"We saw some Indians across the river from us, and Daddy was afraid they might try to steal our animals. So that night he hung all of mama's pots and pans all over the mules."

"Did it work?"

"Sure did. The rattling and clanging kept us, the Indians, and all the animals for miles and miles awake all night."

They both laughed. Then Dorie said, "Dave, how long have you been doing this?"

"Doing what?"

"You know, working on this wagon train."

"This is my third trip."

"Do you like it? I mean your work."

"It's a livin.'"

"Do you ever think about settling down. You don't want to do this kind of work forever, do you?"

"I never had a reason to do anything else, that is 'til now."

"Until now?"

"I mean, uh..." Daggett's face reddened. "I guess I've never met anyone I'd be willin' to change for, 'til I met you."

Dorie blushed. "You'd do that for me?"

"Well...yes, but I'm not sure I can. I'm no farmer, and I don't like workin' for someone else."

"You work for Mr. Moorehouse."

"I know, but that's different. Being a scout, you're more or less your own boss." Daggett picked up a pebble and tossed it into the stream. "Dorie, I don't know anything else except what I'm doin' now."

Dorie stared at Daggett, started to say something, and then began gathering up the leftovers and putting them in the picnic basket. "We'd better be gettin' back," she said.

Daggett picked up the basket, and they walked in silence back to the wagons. When they arrived at the Seymour wagon, Daggett said, "Thanks for the picnic, Dorie, it was nice."

"You're welcome," she said without looking up. She took the basket from him and walked away.

Daggett made his way back to the supply wagon, thinking about what had just happened. He was angry with himself for saying what he did. But it was the truth. Scouting was all he knew. But if he was being honest, then why did he feel so damned miserable. "Dammit," he muttered. He knew Dorie was right. He couldn't do this kind of work forever. He looked up and saw Ellie coming his way.

"Wait up, Dave," she called out. "How are you feeling?"

"Whatta you mean, how am I feelin'?"

"Red Eagle told me you were sick."

"That's funny. He told me that *you* were sick."

"Oh that boy. He asked me how I was, and I told him that I'd felt better. But what about you?"

"I'm fine, Ellie. I just wasn't in the mood for talkin', that's all."

"Well I'm glad. Oh, Andy was looking for you."

"What's he want? Did he say?"

"No, but he seemed concerned. You'd best check with him."

"Thanks Ellie, I will."

Daggett found Moorehouse at the supply wagon. "Ellie said you wanted to see me, Andy. What's up?"

"Looks like we've got ourselves a problem Dave."

"Now what?"

"Seems there's been a rock slide about four miles up the trail.

"How do you know?"

"A couple of fellers came through about an hour ago on their way back to Fort Laramie. They told me."

"Then how'n hell did they get through?"

"No wagon. They was horseback."

Daggett looked around. "Well, it's a little late in the day now. I'll leave first thing in the mornin' and check it out."

"Okay, but get out there early. Leave before sunup so you can find out how much of a problem it's gonna be."

CHAPTER SIXTEEN

Daggett and Red Eagle rode out before daylight. They followed a seldom-used pony path covered with vegetation, bordered by stands of spiny scrub oak trees. This led them to the main trail that wound its way along the Sweetwater. Vines and bushes wet with overnight mist hugged the riverbank. A strong wind rustled the leaves of the huge cottonwoods. At daybreak the trees were mirrored upside-down in the still parts of the stream. Only the wind in the trees and the horse's hooves disturbed the early morning stillness.

Red Eagle broke the silence. "What we do, Dave Daggett, if trail blocked?"

"We unblock it. But let's just hope it's not blocked."

"I say prayer."

"A prayer, who to? The God of blocked trails?"

"No, to Miss Ellie God."

Daggett looked over at him. "To Miss Ellie's God? Whatta you know about Ellie's God?"

"She teach me. I know Lord prayer. You know too?"
"I used to."
"I teach you."
"That's great. You teach me."
"It good you know prayer bad. Miss Ellie say bad if know prayer good."

Daggett reined up. "What the hell are you talkin' about?"

"She say if know prayer good, it just words. She want me think what I say."

"Okay, Red Eagle, the sermons' over."

"Sermon?"

"Forget it. We've got work to do."

Red Eagle bowed his head. "I pray now for blocked trail."

"Yeah, you do that."

The rest of the way the two of them rode in silence, Red Eagle thinking about his prayer, while Daggett's thoughts were mostly about Dorie.

As they rounded a turn in the trail, Daggett reined in his horse. "What the hell?"

"What wrong?" asked Red Eagle.

"Nothin'," said Daggett. "That's what's wrong. This is where the rock slide is supposed to be."

"No here rock slide."

"This is where those two fellers told Andy the trail was blocked."

"That good. Prayer work. We go back now?"

"No, we don't go back now. We'll go a little further just to make sure."

Andy Moorehouse took off his hat and slammed it against the side of the wagon. "Why in hell would those two yahoos tell a lie like that? Now we've lost three hours of daylight."

"Thought they were pullin' somethin' funny I suppose," said Daggett. "How old were they?"

"Old enough to know better."

"Just be glad they were lyin'. 'Course there'll be no livin' with Red Eagle now."

"Why's that?"

"Oh, Ellie's tryin' to make a Christian out of him. He said a prayer, and now he thinks that's why there werent no rockslide. Gullible little shit."

Moorehouse grinned. "Makes you sorta wonder though, huh?"

"No, it don't make me wonder."

"What if he's right?"

"Aw C'mon, Andy, you can't believe that, not for a minute."

"It don't matter whether I believe it or not. What matters is that Red Eagle believes it." Then Moorehouse chuckled. "You'll have to be sure and tell Ellie. Let her know what a grand job she's doin'."

Daggett climbed on his horse. "I've gotta go, but do me a favor, Andy. Forget we even had this talk."

Moorehouse stood grinning as Daggett rode off.

Daggett headed for Ellie's wagon. Red Eagle was waiting for him.

"Where's Ellie?" asked Daggett.

"She with Mr. Bick..., uh,..., Mr. Uh..."

"Bickham?"

Red Eagle's face lit up. "Yes, Mr. Bickham. He hurt foot."

"Good."

Red Eagle frowned. "It good he hurt foot?"

"No. It not good he hurt foot— Dammit, now you've got me

talkin' like you. I mean it's good that Ellie's not here because I ain't got time to bat the breeze. Now get your horse and let's go." Daggett looked around. "Hurry up," he said. He knew Red Eagle would have told Ellie about how he had cleared the trail with a prayer. He wanted to get away before Ellie showed up.

The trail meandered along the bank of the Sweet Water. An hour later it left the prairie and headed toward some foothills. The trail was three wagons wide, but that wouldn't slow things down much.

He and Red Eagle had traveled about two miles when black clouds formed in the southwest, and the sky darkened. Daggett reined up and turned to Red Eagle. "Ride back to the train. Tell Andy Moorehouse that it's gonna be a short day, that there's bad weather movin' in."

"What you do, Dave Daggett?"

"I'll wait for the train on the other side of this hill, I'm sure we'll be back on flat land there."

"I go tell now." said Red Eagle, "and I say prayer."

"Wait a minute," Daggett yelled. "Forget the prayer. Now tell me what you're gonna tell Andy Moorehouse."

"I say, short day. Bad weather come, so I say prayer. Dave Daggett wait far side hill."

"Okay, Parson, go on."

"What?"

"Just go!"

Daggett didn't like the looks of the area where they would be camping. It was flat all right, but if it poured rain there'd be flooding for sure.

When the train showed up, Daggett caught Moorehouse before he circled the wagons. "Andy, I don't know about this campin' spot. If there's a downpour, we could be in trouble. You sure you wanna circle up here?"

Moorehouse studied the sky. "I don't know, Dave, It looks like it may pass west of us. Dammit, we got a late start this mornin', and it's gonna soon be dark. No, we'll stay right here. I've made the decision, and that's it." Then Moorehouse stood up in the stirrups and waved his hat in a circle.

Daggett usually slept under the supply wagon, but with the threat of rain he climbed inside and squeezed in between a barrel and a box, leaned back against the side of the wagon and tried to sleep. He had just dozed off when the storm hit. A blowing rain battered the canvas cover most of the night. Just before dawn the rain let up. Daggett started to check outside, but decided to wait until daylight. But after fifteen minutes, curiosity got the best of him. He climbed over the side of the wagon and stepped off the wheel spokes into knee-deep mud and water.

Daggett heard someone sloshing along coming his way. It was Andy Moorehouse. "Good, mornin' Andy."

"I don't wanna hear it, Dave."

"Hear what?"

"You know damned well what. That I told you so crap, that's what."

"What the hell you talkin' about? I cant say 'good mornin' to you?"

"You never did before. Anyway, what the hell's good about it?"

"Look, Andy, I ain't gonna fight with you. I've gotta find my horse. That is if he ain't drowned."

"That's exactly what I was talkin' about," Moorehouse yelled. "Well you won't be needin' your horse today. You ain't goin' nowhere. It's gonna take everybody here to get these wagons outta this muck."

Daggett looked around at the wagons. In the early morning light he could see what a mess they had to deal with. "Okay, Andy, whatta you got in mind? Whatta we gonna do?"

"Well, for them wagons that can't make it we'll double team 'em with oxen. And them with mules, well, they'll have to wait'll last. Get hold of Luke, Jake, and Emmett. Tell 'em to spread the word. But first tell them that's got mules not to hitch up their animals. They can help where they can with the other wagons, then we'll come back with oxen to pull 'em out. Dammit, this is gonna take us the whole day."

The wagon train came alive. Men yelled orders and cursed. Some chopped down small trees to make poles that were slipped under the rear axles, then men would heave the end of the poles upward to lever those wagons from the muck and get them moving. It was hard work. Men were soaking wet and exhausted, but by noon all of the wagons had been moved to high ground. Moorehouse was elated. Things had gone better than expected. But he knew the day was over, and they'd lost another day. Everybody had earned the right to dry out and rest up. He put out the word that the train would pull out next morning at first light. He could see what a mess they had to deal with. Daggett leaned against the supply wagon, trying to clean the mud from his boots when Nate Williams showed up. "Hey, Dave, Andy wants to see you"

"What about?"

"Hell, I don't know. I suppose…Aw hell, I ain't even gonna suppose. You'll have to find out for yourself."

"Nate, sometimes you don't make a helluva lot of sense. You know that?"

"Look, I'm just deliverin' a message. You can do what you wanna."

"I'm sorry, Nate. Guess I'm just a little tired."

"Ain't we all?"

Daggett had avoided Andy Moorehouse all day. Now he was too tired to start fighting with him, but when he walked up, Andy grinned and held out a cup of coffee to him.

"Whatta you want, Andy?"

"Nothin' in particular. Just wanted to make sure you wasn't intendin' to ride out this afternoon. No need to. Hell, you're as tired as the rest of us. They ain't nothin' out on that trail that won't wait 'til mornin'."

"I wasn't gonna ride out today."

"Good. Look, Dave, I wanna talk to you about what happened this mornin'. I was outta line. Then he grinned and said, "All that rain must've made me a little crazy."

"Yeah, me too. But it wasn't as bad as it might've been."

"Thank God. Oh, I found out a little about those two yahoos that lied about the rockslide. They was kicked off a wagon train."

"How do you know?"

"Old John Roper had trouble with his wagon and was laggin' back about two miles. Seems they shared a bottle of rot-gut with him. Guess it loosened their tongues a little. John told me this mornin'."

"Too bad he didn't tell you before. Why'd they get kicked off the wagon train?"

"They didn't say. But it must've been something pretty bad. The wagon master kept their wagon and everything in it."

"Good. Sounds like they might've been thieves. I hope the bastards had somethin' worth somethin' in their wagon."

"Yeah, I suppose they was tryin' to take their anger out on us, make us pay for what that other wagon master did to 'em."

"Well," said Daggett, straightening his hat. "Think I'll have a look around." As Daggett walked away, Moorehouse grinned and yelled, "Give my best to Mr. Seymour."

CHAPTER SEVENTEEN

Daggett and Dorie walked hand in hand away from the wagons. They both spoke at the same time.

"Dave, when will..."

"Dorie, I want..."

"I'm sorry," said Dorie. "Go ahead."

"No, go on. What were you gonna say?"

Dorie smiled and continued. "I was going to ask you when are we going to get to South Pass."

"Too soon. Barring anymore problems, four, maybe five days."

"What do you mean, too soon?"

Dave's face reddened. "I mean, uh, well, the closer we get to Fort Bridger the sooner you'll be leaving this trail."

Dorie smiled. "So?"

"Dang it Dorie You know..."

Dorie reached over and took his hands in hers. "I was only teasing you Dave. I feel the same way."

Daggett looked surprised. "You do?"

"Yes I do." Then she frowned. "But if I remember right, you said you could never give up this job."

Daggett drew a circle in the dirt with the toe of his boot. "That's what I wanted to talk to you about. I've been givin' it a lotta thought. Maybe I could work something out with Andy. Maybe he could find another scout. Maybe he could even..."

She turned Daggett's hands loose. "Maybe, maybe. So maybe we shouldn't be spending so much time together. Maybe you need more time alone to think about what you're going to do, maybe, huh?" She spun around and walked away, leaving Daggett standing with a puzzled look.

"Dammit, Dorie," he yelled, "why are you always fightin' me?"

"I'm not fighting you." She shouted over her shoulder. "You're fighting yourself."

Daggett strolled back to the wagons, keeping well behind Dorie.

"Dave, Dave Daggett."

Lost in his thoughts, Daggett didn't hear Ellie calling his name. She caught up and took him by the arm. He jumped, and turned around.

"Is everything all right with you, Dave?"

"Yeah, why?"

"You didn't hear me calling you?"

"I was just goin' over somethin' in my mind, Ellie. Whatta you want?"

"Red Eagle will meet you out on the trail tomorrow morning."

"What?"

"Well, he says being around so many people all the time is

not good for him. Something about cleansing his inner-self. He rode out about an hour ago." Ellie smiled. "And you know what, Dave? I don't blame him. Sometimes I wish I could just ride away for a day of solitude."

"It don't matter, Ellie. I'm gettin' used to Red Eagle's quirky ways."

"Well I have to check on the Owens' new baby boy," said Ellie, and turned to leave.

"Wait up, Ellie. Can we talk?"

She smiled. "I thought that's what we were doing."

Daggett looked around and said, "You were married. Did you and your husband argue much?"

Ellie looked puzzled. "Some. No more than any other married couple I guess. Why?"

Daggett looked uncomfortable. "Well, You know me and Dorie Seymour's been seeing each other, and…well…it seems like all we do is argue. Every time I try to tell her how I feel, we get in an argument."

Ellie looked at Daggett for a minute and asked, "What do you argue about?"

"Well, a while back I told her I didn't know if I could leave this job and settle down. She got mad. Then today I told her that maybe I could, and she got mad all over again. I don't know what to think."

Ellie thought a minute. "You know something, Dave? Perhaps the word 'maybe' is what she doesn't like."

"Ellie, I really like her, and I'd leave this job to be with her."

"Then tell her that."

"But Ellie I don't know nothin' about Oregon. I don't even know what's up there. I'm no farmer. What would I do? It's scary."

"I don't know, Dave. I'm afraid I can't help you. That's something you're going to have to figure out for yourself. But if you really want to make a life with her, then the two of you are going to have to sit down and talk. Not argue. Talk."

Daggett said, "Thanks Ellie" and walked away.

"Dave," Ellie shouted.

Daggett turned around. "Yeah?"

Ellie began laughing. "When you talk to Dorie, maybe you shouldn't use the word maybe."

Daggett rode out at daylight; two miles later he saw Red Eagle sitting on his horse waiting for him.

"Good morning, Dave Daggett."

"Mornin', Red Eagle. Did you get your inner-self cleansed?"

"I feel much good. Many people crowd self out."

Daggett dismounted and started tightening his saddle cinch. "Yeah, that's bad when you get yourself crowded outta yourself."

"No funny, Dave Daggett. It true. Many people steal self."

Daggett finished adjusting the cinch and swung up into the saddle. "Well, while we've still got ourselves, whatta you say let's take ourselves on down this trail, huh?"

"No funny I say, Dave Daggett."

"Wasn't meant to be." Daggett looked over at Red Eagle, and wondered what would happen to him when this journey was over? He's so damned gullible. Someone's gotta look out for him. Maybe, he thought, Red Eagle could go back with Andy and the boys. He'd talk to Andy about it. Daggett remembered the time he told Andy that he and Ellie oughta get married and adopt Red Eagle, and laughed out loud.

Red Eagle jerked around. "I said no funny, Dave Daggett."

Daggett reined his horse to a stop. "Tell me Red Eagle, whatta you aim to do after we get where we're goin'?"

Red Eagle thought a minute. "I go see big lake."

"Big lake?"

"Miss Ellie say lake so big, no see across."

"Oh, you mean the ocean?"

"Yes, ocean lake. You see?"

"No."

"I go see."

"After you see the ocean then you'll go home?"

Red Eagle spurred his horse on. "I no never go home."

"Why not?"

"I cannot."

Daggett rode in front of Red Eagle and stopped him. "Dammit why can't you go home? Tell me," he yelled. "Now!"

Red Eagle lowered his eyes "I steal Gray Cloud knife."

Daggett stared at him. "Well hell, give it back."

Red Eagle began fumbling with the horse's bridle. "I no have knife."

"What'd you do, lose it?"

"No. Man I cut take knife."

Daggett thought a minute. "Joe Perkins has got your knife? I'll get it back for you."

"He give you knife?"

"Your damned right he will."

"Thank you, Dave Daggett."

"Then will you go home?"

"After I see ocean lake."

"Well what's so damned important about seein' the ocean? It's just a great big bunch of water. Hell, you can't even drink it."

"Miss Ellie say by Ocean Lake is something called seashell. She say they all kind…uh…what you call?"

"Pretty?"

"No. How look. She say all different."

Daggett tried to figure out what Red Eagle was talking about. "All different, all different," he mumbled. "Shoot," he yelled, "you mean different shapes."

"Yes," cried Red Eagle. "Miss Ellie say no two same."

Daggett watched a hawk soaring high above them, then turned back to Red Eagle. "If you know what they look like then why go and see 'em?"

Red Eagle lowered his eyes. "If I give knife back Gray Cloud and tell about ocean lake and show seashell, maybe they no stay mad with me."

Daggett decided he'd talk to Ellie. Maybe she'd have some influence on Red Eagle. After all, she's the one who filled his head with ocean lakes and seashells.

CHAPTER EIGHTEEN

Ellie stood next to her wagon talking to a lady and a small boy. Daggett rolled a cigarette and waited. When the lady left with the boy, Daggett approached the wagon. "Just a minute, Ellie," he yelled, "I want to talk to you."

"Oh, hello Dave. What can I do for you?"

Daggett looked around. "Where's Red Eagle?"

"He's taking care of the mules. Why? Is something wrong?"

"There sure is. You've been tellin' him all about the ocean, and now he's hell bent on goin' to see it. You know he can't go wandering off all by hisself."

"He told you that?"

"He sure did. You've gotta talk to him."

Ellie picked up her medical bag and put it in the wagon. "I think you're over-reacting, Dave. We've got a long way to go yet. Chances are he'll forget all about it. You know how boys are. Remember when he was going to go to Ireland?"

"Yeah, but that was different. He couldn't get to Ireland, but he can get to the ocean if he's a mind to."

"Okay, Dave, I'll have a talk with him."

There was a loud commotion a few wagons away, people hollering, and a woman screaming. Ellie shaded her eyes trying to see what was happening.

"I've gotta go, Ellie, and see what's goin' on." Daggett turned to leave and Ellie yelled, "Since when did you become so concerned with Red Eagle's welfare, Dave?" He didn't answer.

Daggett could see a crowd around the Dutton wagon. Mrs. McGill ran up to him. "Do something, Mister Daggett. Jimmy's got a knife. He threatened to kill his Dad. Now he's holding it to his own throat."

He pushed his way through the crowd and saw Moorehouse trying to talk Jimmy Dutton into putting the knife away. Daggett walked up next to Moorehouse.

Jimmy was crying. Daggett smiled and said, "Hi Jimmy. Whatta you doin'?"

Jimmy yelled, "You stay back Mister Daggett or I swear I'll use this knife."

"Hey," said Daggett. "You don't wanna do that. You got any idea what it feels like to get cut with a knife?" Rolling up his sleeve, he walked toward Jimmy. "Here look where I got cut once."

Jimmy lunged at Daggett. He swung the knife downward, catching Daggett in the chest. Daggett staggered backwards and fell down. A shot rang out, and Jimmy holding his leg crumpled to the ground. Moorehouse and two other men pounced on him.

Ellie heard the shot and came running. She shoved her way through the crowd and knelt down next to Jimmy.

Moorehouse took her by the shoulders. "Forget him, Ellie.

Look after Dave. Jimmy stabbed him in the chest."

"Oh my God," she muttered, and hurried over to Daggett. "Someone get his shirt off," she cried, "and do it gently." Once his shirt was off, she looked him over, then stood up. "What's going on here, Dave? You haven't been stabbed."

"I haven't?"

"No. All you've got is a bruise on your chest. "

Moorehouse bent over Daggett. "Dammit I saw him get stabbed."

"I can't argue with you now, Andy. I've got to help Jimmy."

Jimmy Dutton lay on his back. His pants had been removed.

"Is he gonna be awright?" asked Nate Williams. "I didn't wanna hurt him, but he didn't give me no choice. I had to do somethin'."

"Let me have a look." After examining the wound, Ellie said, "You're going to be fine, Jimmy. You just lost a little flesh off of your thigh. You're lucky Nate's such a bad shot. I'll bandage it up and give you something for the pain."

"Then he's gonna be awright, huh?" Nate asked.

Ellie gave Nate a smile. "He's fine, Nate. You can quit worrying." Then she turned back to Jimmy. "I'll look in on you later."

Jimmy reached over and took Ellie by the arm. "I don't know what got into me, Miss Ellie. I'm sorry."

Ellie stared at him. "You should be saving your sorrys for your Daddy and Dave Daggett."

Moorehouse was talking to Daggett. When Ellie walked up, he asked, "How's Jimmy?"

"Nothing serious, he's going to be all right. Look, Andy, I think you'd better tell the Duttons to keep a close watch on Jimmy."

"Why? You think he still wants to hurt his Dad?"

"No. I'm more concerned about him harming himself."

Ellie picked up Daggett's shirt, and started to give it to him. She felt something heavy in the pocket, and took it out. It was a smooth flat stone with a chip in the center. She held up the stone and smiled at Daggett. "Looks like this is your lucky day, Dave. What were you doing with this rock in your shirt pocket?"

"Well I'll be damned," said Daggett. "Red Eagle gave me that stone. Said it would bring me luck." Then he moaned. "Ellie, please do me a favor. Don't tell Red Eagle about this. If you do, I'll never hear the last of it."

Ellie picked up Daggett's shirt, looked it over, and said "Sure, Dave, whatever you say." Then she smiled, pitched Daggett his shirt, and walked away.

Daggett looked over at Moorehouse. "She's gonna tell him, ain't she."

"Oh yeah."

"Dave, Dave."

Daggett looked around. It was Dorie. She ran up to him. "Oh Dave, some people told me that you got cut with a knife. They said you got stabbed in the chest."

Daggett stood up. "No, no, Dorie, It was all a mistake. I'm fine."

"Oh thank God," she said, and put her arms around his waist.

Moorehouse pushed back his hat, grinned and said, "There's something I've gotta take care of. I'll see you later, Dave."

Daggett took Dorie by the shoulders and held her at arms length. "Hey, I thought you was mad at me."

She frowned. "I was, but when I heard that you were hurt, I…well…it scared me."

Daggett grinned. "Well, well, so you weren't mad at me after all."

Dorie glared at Daggett. "I wasn't, but I am now. You're…you're I don't know what." She whirled around and walked off.

Daggett caught up with her and blocked her way. "Wait a minute, Dorie, I'm sorry, I shouldn't have made sport of how you felt. I don't know what gets into me sometimes."

She scowled at him. "Neither do I."

"Look, Dorie, you and your folks will be splittin' off this trail for Oregon before too much longer, so lets not waste what time we'll have together, fightin'. Whatta you say?"

"Fine with me, but sometimes you're so…"

"Dorie!"

She smiled. "Okay, Dave, let's try. Truce?"

"Truce." Daggett put an arm around her shoulders and walked with her.

When they arrived at the Seymour wagon, Dorie's mom, Edna, ran over to them. "Oh Mister Daggett, we heard you were in a knife fight. Are you all right?"

"It weren't nothin', ma'am. I'm fine."

"When Dorie heard you were hurt, she tore out of here like she was shot out of a canon."

"Mama!"

"Well, it's true. Anyway, since when is it wrong to be concerned about a friend. I swear, I don't know why you young people are so afraid to show your feelings."

Daggett looked over at Dorie and smiled. Dorie glared at him.

Mrs. Seymour spoke up. "Mister Daggett, why don't you have supper with us."

"Why, uh, that sounds good, Ma'am, but I oughta warn you though, I'm pretty hungry."

"Well," said Mrs. Seymour, "I've learned over the years that I'd rather feed two hungry men than one man that says he ain't hungry."

Daggett laughed. "What time's supper?"

Mrs. Seymour looked at Dorie and back at Daggett. "Give us an hour."

An hour later when Daggett showed up, the two women had the food laid out on the wagon's tailgate.

Mrs. Seymour handed Daggett a plate, and said, "Help yourself. Take what you like and leave what you don't like."

"No problem there," said Daggett. "It all looks good."

During the meal, Mister Seymour turned to Daggett and asked, "Tell me Dave, do you enjoy your job as wagon scout? What with all the travelin' I mean."

"He loves it." Dorie broke in.

Mister and Mrs. Seymour stared at Dorie. Then Mister Seymour continued. "It seems to me to be an awfully tough life, being on the trail all the time, and never knowin' what or who you might run into."

Daggett pushed aside his plate. "It's only once a year. Then I have a good amount of free time in between trips. It's not so bad."

Seymour took a sip of coffee and asked, "You ever think of doin' something else?"

"He don't know nothing else," said Dorie.

"Dorie!" said Mrs. Seymour, "mind your manners."

Mister Seymour gave Dorie a puzzled look, then turned back to Daggett. "You might oughta think about Oregon. It's a new country openin' up there, and I understand that the Willamette Valley has good fertile land for farmin'."

"He's no farmer," said Dorie.

Mrs. Seymour began picking up the plates. She glared at Dorie, and said, "Get the coffee, girl."

When Daggett and Amos finished their coffee they stood next to the wagon smoking. "Look, Dave," said Seymour, "about South Pass, how big a problem is it gonna be? My wagon's loaded pretty heavy. I sure hope I won't have to offload anything, especially any of Edna's furniture."

Daggett looked at the wagon. "You'll make it fine, Amos. I know you hear a lotta stories 'bout South Pass, how high it is and all that, but it's not that bad. Sure it's high, but it ain't steep. Hell, if it weren't for the cold air and a few scattered patches of snow, you'd never know you was passin' over it."

Mister Seymour let out a long breath. "Boy am I glad to hear that. 'Cause if we had to unload anything, Edna would throw out our food before she'd get rid of any of the furniture."

Dorie and her mother were washing dishes. Mrs. Seymour squeezed out the dishrag. "Dorie, what in the world has got into you?"

"What, Mama?"

"You know good and well what, the way you treated Dave Daggett at supper. I thought you liked him."

Dorie set some dishes in a box and said, "I do like him, Mama, but what I said is true. He's never going to settle down."

Mrs. Seymour stared at her. "Not with you, that's for sure. Not after the way you acted at supper."

"I only repeated what he'd already told me."

Mrs. Seymour smiled. "Honey, young men say a lotta things they don't mean. When your father was young he was no different. Before we were married he decided he was gonna go back east and get rich workin' in the coalmines. Now that was a dumb idea."

"How come he changed his mind?"

Mrs. Seymour smiled. "He didn't, I changed it for him."

"Oh, how'd you manage that?"

"Never you mind, girl. Help me with this box."

CHAPTER NINETEEN

Early the next morning, Daggett rode up to Ellie's wagon. Red Eagle was sitting on his horse waiting and smiling from ear to ear. "Good morning, David."

"Good morning what?"

"I say good morning, David."

"That's what I thought you said. What's with this David stuff?"

"Miss Ellie tell me your name, David. She say that your true name."

"Yeah. What else did she tell you?"

Still smiling, Red Eagle said, "She tell me maybe I no tell you what she tell me."

Daggett gave Red Eagle an angry look, leaned over and said, "I tell you I know what Ellie tell you maybe no tell me. Now wipe that silly grin off your face and let's get on down the trail." He jerked his horse around.

"Wait," cried Red Eagle. Show me lucky stone."

"I threw it away," Daggett shouted over his shoulder.

"No! No!" Red Eagle yelled.

Daggett reined up. "Look, I don't wanna hear anymore about that damned rock. Now lets get movin'. We've gotta make it to South Pass today."

Red Eagle took out the pistol that Daggett had given him and threw it as far as he could.

"What the hell are you doing?" Daggett yelled.

"I give you lucky stone for pistol. You no want stone, I no want pistol."

Daggett rode over, found the pistol, looked it over, put it in his saddlebag. "Suit yourself," he said. "Now lets go."

The two of them rode in silence the rest of the day. When Daggett spoke, Red Eagle would shake his head or nod for yes or no but would say nothing.

Late that afternoon they arrived at South Pass and dismounted. Daggett said, "The train will camp here tonight. Then the wagons will get an extra early start in the mornin'. It's gonna be a long day tomorrow, and cold. You'd better see if Ellie can dig up some warm clothes for you."

Red Eagle slid off his horse, still not speaking.

"Ain't you interested in crossin' over South Pass?" asked Daggett. "Don't you wanna know what it's gonna be like?"

Red Eagle shook his head.

"Have it your way."

The two of them spent the next two hours waiting for the wagon train's arrival in silence.

When the train showed up, Daggett sought out the Seymour wagon. Amos Seymour was unhitching the oxen. "Hey, Dave," he yelled, "I thought we was gonna get to South Pass today?"

Daggett smiled. "We're here, Amos. This is it."

"This is South Pass?"

"Sure is. I told you it was a gentle rise. Hell, it must be fifteen, maybe twenty miles wide, just one great big valley. Biggest problem for the next few days is gonna be keepin' warm. You'd better have the Misses rustle up some winter clothes. Moorehouse'll pass the word around, but I thought I'd let you know."

Mrs. Seymour and Dorie came around from the back of the wagon. "What's this about the misses?" Mrs. Seymour asked.

Daggett tipped his hat. "I was just tellin' Amos that everybody'll have to dress warm for the next few days."

Dorie looked around. "Is it really going to get that cold? That's hard to believe."

"Yeah it is," said Daggett. "Believe it."

"Come on," Mrs. Seymour said to Dorie, "We'll have to dig through the trunk. I packed all the winter clothes in the bottom. Never thought they'd be needed."

Mister Seymour turned to Daggett. "How longs it gonna take to get over this pass and down the other side?"

Daggett rubbed his chin, and said, "Oh, four, maybe five days, a couple days up this side and about the same goin' down the other side. That is barring any problems."

Early the next morning, Daggett and Red Eagle were on their way. Red Eagle was still not talking. Daggett reined up. "Listen, Red Eagle, I'm really gettin' tired of your poutin'. You know I can do this job by myself. If you're gonna act like a baby I'd just soon not have you along."

Red Eagle lowered his eyes, then looked back at Daggett. "What you want me do?"

I want you to quit actin' like a baby, and quit your damned poutin'."

"What mean, poutin'?"

Daggett glared at Red Eagle. "Like I said, actin' like a baby."

"All right, David, I no pout."

"And don't call me David."

"All right Dave Daggett."

Even though the two of them had more or less settled their differences, there wasn't much talking. Around mid afternoon they stopped and dug out warm clothing. Daggett put on a fur lined sheep skin coat. Red Eagle had a sweater and a rawhide jacket that Ellie had gotten from two ladies.

Daggett pitched Red Eagle an extra pair of gloves. "Here put these on."

"How long we wear these?" Red Eagle asked.

Daggett pulled on his gloves and said, "Four days or so. When we cross the salt flats you'll be wishin' for some of this cold weather."

Red Eagle put on the gloves, then held out his hands, turning them back and forth, studying the gloves. "How far we from top South Pass?"

Daggett turned up his coat collar. "I don't know for sure, maybe six or seven miles."

"Why we no go on top?"

Daggett grinned. "Why, ain't this cold enough for you?"

"It more cold on top?"

"Yeah, Red Eagle, it more cold on top."

When the wagons arrived, fires were built, not only for cooking but to keep warm. Folks had on their winter clothes, and stood around the fires.

Daggett headed for the Seymour wagon with two bouquets of wild flowers he had found growing next to a patch of snow. Dorie and her folks were standing around their fire eating. He took the flowers from behind his back and handed them to the two women.

"Oh, Dave," Mrs. Seymour said, "They're beautiful. Where in the world did you find them?"

Dorie blushed and said, "Thank you, Dave"

Daggett said, "They grow wild up here. I don't know how they do it. Seems like it'd be too cold for flowers."

Mrs. Seymour held them out and studying them. "I wonder what kind they are?" They look somewhat like lilies."

"They are," said Daggett. Not that I'd know, but on my last trip through here there was a man who studied flowers and plants. I forget what he called himself."

"A botanist?" said Mrs. Seymour.

"Yeah, it could be, I'm not sure. He showed me some other flowers too. He called them Indian Paintbrush. I didn't see any of them today though. Anyway, he said these are avalanche lilies."

"Well they sure are pretty. This is very thoughtful of you, Mr. Daggett."

Dorie held the bouquet to her face. "They smell wonderful. Thank you Dave,"

"I don't get any?" Mr. Seymour said, grinning.

"Dang," Daggett said, "I should've picked more." They all laughed. "Well I think I'll go get under some covers."

As he left, the two women thanked him again for the flowers.

That night Daggett slept inside the supply wagon, not under it as he normally did. In the middle of the night he was awakened by a hailstorm. The strong wind buffeted the wagon so hard he feared it might turn over. Hail pelted the canvas with a fury. Then something slammed into the wagon. At first he thought that maybe a tree had fallen on it. He pulled the jacket over his head to protect himself from the hail and scrambled out of the wagon. Some of the livestock had broken loose and were stampeding through the area. He couldn't see well with the coat over his head. Before Daggett could get back inside, an ox ran into him, slamming him into the side of the wagon. He managed to roll underneath it where he lay for two hours, with a large gash on his forehead, and his ribs aching. "*Christ*, he thought, *Jimmy Dutton tries to stab me, a damned ox plows into me. What the hell else can happen?*" Finally, the storm abated, and Daggett could hear people stirring about. He began yelling for help. Every time he yelled it hurt his ribs. At last, a man heard him and came over.

"Help me out of here," Daggett told him.

"What happened to you?" the man asked.

"An ox ran into me. I think I may have some broke ribs. Give me a hand."

The man reached out his hand, then drew it back. "Maybe I'd better get that doctor woman"

"No, dammit help me out of here."

"I don't think so," the man said. "Movin' you might make things worse. I once knew a man what had some broke ribs, and one of 'em punctured something inside him. Damned near kilt him. I'd better get that doctor woman to take a look at you first."

"No," Daggett groaned, but the man left.

Fifteen minutes later Ellie showed up with Red Eagle. "Well, what have you gotten yourself into now Dave? Ned Lewis said you were over here lying under the supply wagon hurt bad."

"Aw he don't know what he's talkin' about. A damned ox ran me down, knocked me into the wagon. I had to crawl under here to get outta the way of the rest of 'em. I'm fine."

"Oh, Okay, then Red Eagle and I will be on our way. Bye."

"Hold on a minute," Daggett said.

Ellie turned around. "What's that? Did you say something, Dave?"

"All right, Ellie. I need a little help gettin' out from under here."

Ellie bent down and said, "where are you hurting?"

"My right side. I think maybe I've got some broke ribs. I'll be fine once I'm on my feet. It just hurts when I try to move out from under here."

"Okay, Dave, Lie on your back." Then she turned to Red Eagle. "Get down there and get him under the arms, lace your fingers across his upper chest and drag him out. Don't touch his sides."

Red Eagle did as he was told. With a lot of moaning and groaning by both of them, Red Eagle finally got Daggett out from under the wagon. Then, with Ellie's help they got him to his feet.

"Dave," Ellie said, "You've got a good size cut on your forehead. Let's go to my wagon. I'll take care of it and examine your ribs."

Ellie patched up Daggett's head, and determined that he had two broken ribs. She wrapped tape tight around his upper torso. "Now, Dave I want you to listen to me. You're going to have to take it easy for a few days. That means staying off your horse. You've got to keep those ribs immobile, give them a chance to heal. They could do some bad damage to your insides. Do you understand?"

"Dammit, Ellie I can't do that. I've got a job to do."

Ellie smiled. "Oh I think you can. You'll see."

"Well, we ain't goin' nowhere today anyway. We've gotta get these wagons repaired. Damn, look at 'em. Some of 'em has hardly any canvas left. Not to mention it's gonna take the rest of the day to round up all the mules and oxen."

"Just the same, a day's not going to help you. I want you to take it easy, and I want to see you tomorrow morning, Okay?"

"Awright, Ellie."

After Daggett left, Red Eagle smiled at Ellie and said, "I glad Dave Daggett hurt self."

Ellie stopped and stared at Red Eagle. "Why, Red Eagle, what a terrible thing to say."

Red Eagle said, "If he no get hurt, I never know he keep lucky stone."

"What in the world are you talking about?"

"He say to me he throw stone away, but when I pull him out wagon I feel stone in shirt pocket. He keep stone. I glad."

"Well after what happened to him last night, maybe he should have thrown it away."

"What you say Miss Ellie? I know understand."

Ellie saw the disappointment in Red Eagle's face. "I'm sorry, Red Eagle, You misunderstood me. I said after what happened last night, it's a good thing he didn't throw it away. You know what, Red Eagle, he could have been killed last night. It's a good thing he kept that lucky stone. It probably saved his life."

"I much glad," said Red Eagle, smiling.

That afternoon, Dorie and her mother heard about Daggett being injured, and headed for the supply wagon to see him. Daggett was leaning against the wagon wheel with a cup of water, taking one of the pain remedies that Ellie had given him. Dorie rushed over to him. "Dave, we heard that you got trampled by an ox. You're all right, aren't you?"

Daggett smiled at her. "Yeah, I'm just fine. I'm glad you...I mean thanks for caring."

Dorie frowned. "Well sure I care. Why shouldn't I?"

"I'm sorry, Dorie. Gosh, it seems like I say that a lot to you."

"Well I should thi..."

Mrs. Seymour broke in. "Here Dave we brought you a piece of cake."

Daggett took the cake. "Gee, that's awfully nice of you two. Thanks."

"Enjoy it," said Mrs. Seymour. She smiled, "I sure hope that ox that ran over you wasn't one of ours."

"It was."

Mrs. Seymour stared at him. "Oh my."

Daggett started laughing, then stopped, and grabbed his side. "I was only teasin'. I don't know who the ox belonged to, and I don't care. It don't matter. You can't blame them animals for getting spooked in that storm."

"Well," said Mrs. Seymour, "we won't bother you any more. I hope you get to feeling better."

"I'm fine," said Daggett. "Thanks for comin' by, and thanks for the cake."

The two women turned to leave. "Just a minute," he said. "How did your wagon fair?"

"Not much damage," said Dorie. "Daddy's patching up the canvas now."

"I'm glad to hear that," Daggett said.

"I'm glad you weren't hurt bad, Dave."

"Thanks, Dorie. Can I come by and see you later?"

Dorie smiled. "I'd like that,"

Daggett never got around to visiting Dorie that afternoon. His ribs hurt too much. He made up a pallet under the supply wagon and took it easy the rest of the day.

Early the next morning Daggett tried to mount his horse. He put his foot in the stirrup, but when he took hold of the saddle horn and tried to pull himself up, his ribs hurt too much, so he walked over to Ellie's wagon, leading the horse. Red Eagle was saddled up and waiting.

He frowned at Daggett and said, "What you do here, Dave Daggett?"

"Whatta you mean, what I do here? Whatta you think I do here?"

"Andy Moorehouse say today I go with Mr. Jake Vines. He scout now."

Daggett glared at Red Eagle. "No, he not scout now. Help me up on this horse, and we'll be on our way."

Ellie climbed out of the wagon. "What do you think you're doing, Dave?"

"Good mornin' to you too, Ellie."

Red Eagle took Daggett by the lower leg. "I help on horse."

Daggett pushed him away. "Get away, I don't need no darned help."

"But you say me hel…"

"Get your horse, Red Eagle," he shouted. Then Daggett stuck his foot into the stirrup, grabbed the saddle horn, and with gritted teeth, and silent pain, pulled himself up onto the saddle.

Ellie watched him, then began clapping her hands. "Great performance, Dave. Now I'll get you something for the pain. You're going to need it."

"I'm gonna need it whether I ride this horse or a bouncy wagon."

In fact, I'm better off on this horse. At least I can control him."

"Yes I guess you're right." Ellie said and went back to the wagon. She returned with a small flask. "Here, Dave, take a sip of this."

Daggett took the flask from her, looked it over and asked, "What is it?"

"You wouldn't know if I told you. Take a sip."

He took a small swallow, smacked his lips and said, "Ellie, if you're giving me whiskey I'm gonna need a lot more than a sip."

"It's not whiskey, Dave. Its called laudanum. It's alcohol with just a pinch of opium."

"Opium! I heard somewhere that that stuff makes you crazy."

Ellie recapped the flask and said, "I'll see you tonight, Dave."

"Hold on, Ellie."

She ignored him and walked back to the wagon.

Daggett and Red Eagle traveled slowly, keeping their horses at a steady walk. By early afternoon they reached the top of the pass and dismounted to give the horses a rest. Daggett struggled down from his horse with some difficulty, but refused to let Red Eagle help him.

"Look," said Red Eagle, pointing at snow covered peaks off in the distance.

"That's the Wind River Range," said Daggett. "That one there," he said pointing, "is Fremont's Peak."

"What that, Fremont?" Red Eagle asked.

"It's named after John Fremont. They say he was the first man to come through here. He's supposed to have climbed it."

"Indians no here?"

"Sure they are. Why?"

"Maybe they first here. Maybe they first climb peak."

Daggett looked at Red Eagle. "Yeah, I guess they probably did."

Red Eagle walked over to Daggett. "Dave Daggett."

"What?"

"You give me back pistol now?"

Daggett stared at Red Eagle. "I thought you didn't want it anymore. You threw the damned thing away, remember?"

"That when I think you lucky stone throw away. Now I get pistol."

"Oh. And what makes you think I didn't throw that rock away?"

"I know. That why ox no kill you."

"Oh for cryin' out loud. The pistol's in my saddlebag, get it. But I don't wanna hear no more about that damned so-called lucky stone. Understand?"

Red Eagle took the pistol from the saddlebag, stuck it in his waist band, and said, "I understand, Dave Daggett."

Later that day, dark clouds formed to the southwest. They were a long way off, and Daggett hoped they would stay away. "Okay, Red Eagle," he said, "we'll stop here. I think we can make it the rest of the way down tomorrow." He started to dismount, then turned to Red Eagle. "Give me a hand gettin' down."

Red Eagle dismounted and started over to help. Then stopped. "But you say you no need help."

"I know what I said. Now quit soundin' like Ellie, and give me a hand. All this ridin' today's got me stoved up."

"What stoved up mean?"

"It means I'm stiff. Now get over here and help me."

"You say you do job without me. What if I no here? You stay on horse?"

Daggett glared at Red Eagle. "Get your butt over here, Now!"

CHAPTER TWENTY

Daggett and Dorie stood holding hands, taking in the view of the surrounding mountains. An arbor of evergreens covered them, their tops powdered with snow. Other scattered trees in their late summer colors of scarlet, yellow and orange added to the dazzling scene. Above the timberline the mountains were snow covered. She said, "What a beautiful. Sight."

"This is the Wind River Range. The mountains are something, aren't they? I wish I could've been with you when you were on the very top of the pass." Then he pointed out Fremont's Peak and told her the John Fremont story.

Suddenly she dropped his hand and pointed at a graying sky and two funnel clouds in the distance. "Look Dave, there's a tornado."

Daggett looked at where she was pointing. "Thank goodness it's there and not here."

Staring at the clouds, she said, "You know what those two funnel clouds look like?"

He smiled. "A cow's udder?"

"No, silly, they look like two columns holding up that dark cloud."

"Yeah, by golly they do at that."

Dorie turned and faced him. "Dave, when will we…uh, I mean when does the Oregon Trail branch off from this one?"

"You mean when do we part?"

She looked away and then back at Daggett. "Yes."

"In a few days. After gettin' across South Pass, some Oregon bound folks go on to Fort Hall, but most of 'em stop at Fort Bridger even though it's out of the way. It's a grubby little place, but it's more stocked with supplies than Fort Hall. Your group is gonna stop at Fort Bridger."

Dorie looked surprised. "How do you know that? I mean that we're going to Fort Bridger. Daddy hasn't mentioned it."

Daggett moved a pine cone around with the toe of his boot. "I checked with Andy."

"You checked?"

"Well, yeah."

She put her arm around Daggett and laid her head on his chest "Don't be embarrassed Dave. I'm glad you checked."

"You are?"

"Sure I am. Why is it so hard for us to admit that we like each other?"

"I do like you, Dorie. I like you an awful lot. But I wasn't sure you liked me the same way, you know like, I mean I…"

Dorie put her fingers on his lips. "Quit talking, Dave, and just hold me."

Daggett took her in his arms and kissed her. "Dorie, I think this is gonna be my last trip."

She pushed him away. "You think? You think?"

"I'm sorry, Dorie, I shouldn't have said think. This *is* my last trip."

"Are you sure, Dave. Is that what you really want to do? I want you to be sure."

"Believe me, I'm sure. I'm gonna tell Andy today that he's gonna have to find hisself another scout."

She stood quietly looking off into the distance.

"What's the matter, Dorie? You still don't believe me?"

She turned around "I'm just afraid when you return to Missouri you'll forget all about us."

Daggett took her face in his hands. "Believe me, I could never forget you. Besides, I'm not goin' back to Missouri. As soon as I get these wagons to California I'm headin' for Oregon."

"What about all of your things you left back in Missouri?"

Daggett grinned. "All of what things I left? What? A change of clothes and a Saloon bill?"

"But, Dave, I'm not even sure where we're going. All Daddy knows is that we're going to settle in the Willamette Valley, wherever that is. How will you find us?"

He took her in his arms, held her close and whispered. "I'll find you."

Daggett bent over, holding on to the side of the wagon while Ellie began removing the tape from his upper body. She worked the scissors under the tape and cut across it. Then took the end of each strip, and one at a time started jerking them loose.

Daggett gritted his teeth and let out a moan when each piece came off.

"Damn, Ellie, that hurts like hell."

"It's the only way, Dave. You don't want me to pull it off slow now, do you?"

Daggett took a deep breath. "Go ahead, just get it over with."

When all the tape was off, Daggett said, "Ellie could I talk to you a minute?"

"Sure, Dave, you can talk to me for more than a minute."

He looked around to make sure no one was in hearing distance. "This is serious, Ellie."

"I'm sorry, Dave. What is it you want to talk about?"

"Well, it's Dorie. You know her and her family's goin' to Oregon to the Willamette Valley. Now I ain't told Andy yet, but I aim to head up there when this trips over. And I know he's gonna raise hell."

Ellie stared at Daggett. "Why are you telling me this? I don't know how I can help you."

"I thought maybe you could mention to Andy how you think it's time I quit all this travelin'. How I've got a chance to get married, settle down and raise a family."

Ellie looked down at the ground and back at Daggett. "And what makes you think that he will listen to me?"

"Because he likes you. He'll holler at me, but not at you. The fact is, I think he's a little afraid of you."

Ellie smiled. "I'm flattered, Dave, but, I wouldn't be too sure about that."

They stood in silence for a minute, then Daggett said, "Forget it Ellie. It's probably a crazy idea anyway. After all, this job is all I know. Like I told Dorie, I'm no farmer."

Ellie reached over and put her hand on his shoulder. "Dave, can I give you some advice?"

"Sure, I could use some right now."

A gust of wind kicked up a dust cloud. Ellie turned her back to it, then smoothing her hair with both hands, said, "Look,

Dave, we only have one life to live, and we have to try to make it a happy one. Life is decisions, and we live with the ones we make, good or bad. We don't always make good ones, but we try not to make choices that we'll regret later. Once you've made a decision stick to it, and don't back down. It's your life so do what will make you happy, not necessarily what pleases other people. This is the one time you can be selfish. And never waste your time dwelling on what might've been, or what might be. You know what they say, yesterday is history, tomorrow's a mystery and today is a gift." Then she smiled. "That's why it's called the present."

Daggett stared at her. Then grinned. "I think you just made my mind up. To hell with it. I'm goin' to Oregon." He leaned over and kissed her on the cheek. "Thanks, Ellie."

"What the hell you mean, you're goin' to Oregon?" Moorehouse yelled. "You don't even know where it is." He reached into his saddlebag and pulled out a map, unfolded it and held it out to Daggett. "Here, show me on this map where you're goin'. Show me!"

Daggett pushed the map away. "I knew you'd holler and raise hell. Dammit, Andy, I'm tryin' to do the right thing, can't you see that? I could've just rode off when this trips over and not said nothin'. And the way you're actin' maybe I should've."

Moorehouse shook his head. "You're a scout, not a farmer. You don't know nothin' 'bout farmin', and that's all they do up there. Whatta you gonna do, lead the cows to pasture?" He climbed on his horse and rode off, but yelled back over his shoulder, "You'd better think about what you're doin'."

Daggett watched him ride off. He stood there thinking of Ellie's words of advice, "Make a decision and stick to it. Don't back down".

Daggett and Red Eagle rode along in silence. He looked over at Red Eagle and thought what a wonderful simple life he has. No girl problems, and too damned dumb to worry about anything. Red Eagle turned as if he had read Daggett's thoughts, and asked, "What?"

"Whatta you mean what?"

"You look funny look."

Daggett didn't answer.

"We be at Fort Bridger next?" Red Eagle asked.

"Yeah, today." He'd be glad to get there. He hadn't seen Dorie for two days. Andy had made sure of that, every evening finding something that just had to be done. But the two days they would spend at Fort Bridger would be spent with her, he'd see to that.

Daggett was happy when Fort Bridger came in sight, even though the place looked worse than what he remembered. The sun came out from behind a cloud, but even the soft wash of sunshine couldn't help the appearance of the thrown together shacks.

Red Eagle said, "This good place. I like."

Daggett looked over at him. "You're easy to please."

"You no like?"

"Yes, I no like."

"It got wood house."

"Yeah, if you can call 'em houses. Jim Bridger must put all his money into supplies. He sure as hell don't spend none on anything else."

"I like."

CHAPTER TWENTY-ONE

When the wagons arrived at Fort Bridger and things settled down, Daggett went in search of the Seymour wagon but couldn't find it. He finally located the Guthrie wagon which traveled behind Seymours'.

"Hell," said John Guthrie, "Amos pulled out of line and went on to Fort Hall. Don't you people know who's goin' where?"

"Whatta you mean he went to Fort Hall? He was supposed to come here."

"Well he must've changed his mind."

"That bastard," said Daggett. He jerked his horse around, and went looking for Andy Moorehouse. He found him standing next to the supply wagon. "What the hell are you pullin'?" he yelled as he jumped down from his horse.

Moorehouse frowned. "Whatta you talkin' about?"

"You know damned well what I'm talkin' about. You kept me away from Dorie by workin' hell outta me the last five days, then you don't tell me they pulled out with the other wagons goin' to Fort Hall. Them changin' their mind, was that some of your doin' too?"

"Now just you back up a minute," Andy said. "In the first place, everybody worked long hours the last few days. There was a lot to do after comin' off that mountain; Wheel rims to repair, axles to be greased, and break blocks inspected. Hell, you know what all we had to do. Secondly, do you really think that Amos Seymour and me would go to all the trouble of cookin' up something just to keep you away from that girl? You must have an awful high opinion of yourself. Think about it!"

Daggett stared at the distant blue rimmed mountains. He knew Andy was right, but he was angry and hurt that he didn't get to tell Dorie goodbye.

Moorehouse took off his hat and began fiddling with the band. "Look, Dave, I didn't know Amos changed his mind about goin' on to Fort Hall. He didn't tell me 'till the last minute." He shoved his hat back on. "Now if you're through raisin' hell, I've got somethin' for you." He pulled an envelope out of his shirt pocket. "It's from the girl. She asked me to give it to you." He handed it to Daggett and walked off.

Daggett opened it and read:

> Dear Dave, I'm so mad at Daddy. He never told me he had changed his mind. He said that whatever supplies we need he'd get at Fort Hall, that he didn't want to waste five days by going to Fort Bridger. I was so looking forward to our two days together. It's not fair that we didn't get to say goodbye in person. There is so much I want to say to you, but not in a letter. Please don't forget me. I'll wait for you forever. All my love, Dorie.

The wagon train traveled slowly along the Humboldt River. Grass was plentiful along the stream, but the rest was desert like, with thinly scattered dry grass, sagebrush and prickly pear. One time the wagons were forced away from the river by a deep canyon, but only for a day. After a night on the prairie they rejoined the river late the next morning.

Everyone was happy with the available water and vegetation. But they had been warned about what lay ahead: the Forty-Mile Desert.

Daggett and Red Eagle had traveled along the river for most of the day without speaking. Daggett thinking about his relationship with Moorehouse, and Red Eagle wondering if the silence meant that he had done something wrong.

Daggett hated the falling out with Moorehouse. When they spoke it was awkward, and always about the job at hand. Moorehouse was a good friend, and Daggett knew he had been wrong blaming him for Amos Seymour's leaving the California trail when he did. He wanted to apologize but his pride wouldn't let him. *Dammit*, he thought, *Andy oughta understand. He knew how I felt about Dorie.* He decided he'd talk it out with Moorehouse that evening.

Red Eagle finally broke the silence. "We there almost yet?"

"What?" Daggett asked, coming out of his thoughts.

"I say we there almost yet?"

"Almost where?"

"California."

Daggett stared at him. "No we not there almost yet."

"I be glad when get there."

"Yeah, you and a lotta others. You better enjoy this trip

along the river. When we leave it we cross the forty mile desert."

Red Eagle frowned. "What forty mile desert is?"

"It's two and a half days travel without water or grass."

Red Eagle gave him a puzzled look, then held out his hands, palms up and frowned at Daggett. "If no water no grass why not we go cross forty mile desert with no stop?"

Daggett grinned at him. "That two and a half days *is* without stoppin', except once in awhile to let the animals rest. But not for long."

"What happen to river? Where it go?"

"That's where it peters out."

Red Eagle looked confused. "What peter out?"

"That's where the river dries up. It ends in a dry lakebed. It's called the Humboldt Sink."

"Why it called that?"

"I don't know. It just is."

It was late in the day and long shadows of the riverbank fell across the rippling surface of the water. Daggett said, "This is as good a place as any. We'll wait here for the wagons."

When the wagons arrived and things had settled down, Daggett sought out Moorehouse. He found him talking to Joe Perkins and Nate Williams. Standing to one side while the men talked, Daggett waited for the conversation to end. "I'm tellin' you I seen some Indians this afternoon," Perkins said, "I don't know what they was up to, but I don't like it. You can't trust 'em."

"They're diggers, Moorehouse said.

"Diggers?"

"Yeah, Shoshones. They ain't warlike, but then again they ain't got no qualms about stealin' either. When we get in Paiute country it's a different story."

"Why they called diggers?" Perkins asked.

"Hell I don't know. They just are."

Nate Williams spoke up, They're called diggers 'cause they dig up roots to eat."

Perkins frowned. "They eat roots?"

Williams stared at Perkins. "You ever eat a carrot or sweet potato, Joe?"

"Forget the damned roots," Moorehouse yelled. Then he turned to Nate Williams. "Just to be on the safe side though, you best put out a few more guards tonight. In fact you'd better take care of that right now."

Only after Perkins and Williams left did Daggett approach Moorehouse. "Andy, I wanna talk to you."

Moorehouse whirled around. "I ain't got no time for your personal problems, Dave, If you wanna talk, go see Ellie, she's a good listener. I've got more important things to do."

"Dammit, Andy, this ain't easy for me. I'm tryin' to say I was wrong. I thought I was gonna get to spend some time with Dorie when we got to Fort Bridger. Hell, I didn't even get to tell her goodbye. I was mad and hurt and I had to strike out at somebody. I'm just sorry it was you. Now I've had my say. You can take it any way you want." Daggett turned and walked away.

"Wait just a damned minute," Moorehouse yelled. "You had your say, now I'll have mine."

Daggett stopped and turned around. "Go on."

Moorehouse took off his hat and started fiddling with the brim. "I guess I should've knowed what was eatin' you. But dammit, you ain't the only one that's got a temper. When you came at me like you did, well, I—ah—Look Dave, I'm not very good at this. Whatta you say let's put all this behind us."

Daggett grinned. "Thanks, Andy." He was glad to put it all behind them.

CHAPTER TWENTY-TWO

When the wagon train reached the Humboldt Sink, they found a swampy area of marshy meadows and a few salt lakes, but grass was plentiful. Everyone set about cutting grass for dried hay to be loaded in the wagons for feed, and filling all the containers with water for the long dry stretch across the Forty-Mile desert. Everything that would hold water was filled. Moorehouse had passed the word that they would spend two days at the Sink to rest the animals before tackling the desert.

Daggett decided to take advantage of the free time to sleep but was awakened by Moorehouse early the next morning.

"Dave, I hate to disturb your beauty rest, but we're missin' a couple of wagons."

Daggett stretched and yawned. "Whatta you mean missin' a couple of wagons?"

"Ed Stevens looked me up this mornin'. Told me two wagons pulled out yesterday afternoon, said they was gonna do a little fishin' and would catch up later. But when they never showed up last night and still hadn't showed up this mornin' he got worried and thought he oughta let me know."

Daggett started pulling on his boots. "What the hell was they thinkin' anyway? Who are they? And how many?"

"He ain't sure. Said their names are Ramsey and Guthrie. He thinks there's two men, two women and three kids."

"Dumb bastards."

Moorehouse shook his head. "Yeah I know. I want you and Red Eagle to go back and check on 'em. Find out what the hell's goin' on. But take Nate Williams and Joe Perkins with you."

"Yeah, that's a good idea."

"Dave, be careful. It could be nothin', but you never know."

"Okay, I'd better get Red Eagle. Does Williams and Perkins know they're comin' along?"

"Yeah, they're waitin' for you."

Red Eagle was standing by his horse. He mounted up and asked, "Where we go Dave Daggett?"

"Just something we've gotta check on."

As they rode along, Red Eagle asked, "Why we go same way come?"

"We're missin' a couple of wagons. We gotta find out why." He grinned at Red Eagle, "That why we go same way come."

Williams and Perkins were waiting for them a ways down the trail.

"What the hell was them people thinkin'?" Perkins asked. "It'd serve 'em right if we just went off and left 'em."

Daggett gave him a disdainful look. "The women and kids too, Joe?" Perkins didn't answer.

They traveled back along the river for about three hours when they spotted someone coming their way, on foot. The four of them spurred their horses into a gallop.

"What's your name?" Daggett asked when they rode up.

"Guthrie," he replied. "Boy am I glad to see you."

"You one of them fisherman?" Perkins asked.

Williams swung around in his saddle and said, "Knock it off, Joe."

"What happened?" Daggett asked.

Guthrie glanced at Perkins. "Yeah, we was fishin'. It got late, so we decided to go ahead and cook the fish, and join the wagons at the Sink this mornin'. We knew they was gonna stick around for a couple days. But then—" He began shaking his head.

"But then what?" Daggett asked.

"The damned Indians stole our animals last night."

Perkins grinned at him and said, "No kiddin.'"

Williams turned on Perkins. "Dammit, Joe, shut up."

"Hey," Perkins said, "You may be in charge of the guards, but we ain't on guard duty out here."

"Knock it off, both of you," Daggett yelled. Then asked Guthrie, "Was anyone hurt?"

"No. By the time we realized what was goin' on, they was ridin' off with 'em. We shot at 'em, but—uh—well."

"But what?" Daggett shouted.

"We killed one of the oxen."

Perkins muffled a laugh.

Guthrie glared at Perkins. "Ain't nothin' funny about it. We're stuck out here with two wagons and nothin' to pull 'em with. Everything we own is in them wagons." Then he looked hard at Perkins. "Like I said, ain't nothin' funny about it."

Daggett thought for a minute. "Awright, here's what we're gonna do. Me and Red Eagle will ride back to the wagons and rake up some oxen. I know some of the folks have got extra animals. I'm sure that in a case like this they'll pitch in and help out. The three of you ride back to Guthrie's wagon, I don't like the idea of one man left there watchin' out for those women and kids. Guthrie can ride double with Williams."

"Wait a minute", Williams said, "Maybe Red Eagle oughta stay with us. If there's any trouble we may need all the help we can get."

Daggett looked at Red Eagle and back at Williams. "Red Eagle stays with me." Then he rode over next to Perkins. "Joe, I don't want you needling this guy. I know what he did was dumb, but right now he's got enough to worry about. So keep your damned mouth shut. You hear?"

"Hell, Dave I—"

Daggett grabbed him by the shoulder, "I'd better not hear about any crap takin' place between you and this guy. You got it?"

"Yeah, awright, Dave."

"I sure appreciate what you're doin' for us," Guthrie said. "I know what we done was stupid."

Daggett glanced over at Perkins, and said, "You ain't got a lock on stupidity. Now you'd better get back to your wagon."

Daggett and Red Eagle rode hard back to the wagon train and sought out Moorehouse. After telling him the situation, Moorehouse said, "Well hell, there goes another day lost. We can get 'em some more oxen I'm sure, but if those that loan 'em out need 'em back later, they're obliged to give 'em up with no hassle. I want that understood."

The three of them visited the wagons that had extra animals, and explained the situation. Most turned them down, but they finally came up with two teams of oxen. Moorehouse looked at his pocket watch. "It's three o'clock, How long do you think it'll take to get the oxen back out there?"

Daggett said, "I don't know. I'd guess at least four hours."

"Well, then you'd better get started."

"Hold on, Andy. I'm not makin' that trip again, you're gonna have to get someone else."

"Mind tellin' me why?"

"Because if I spend anymore time around Joe Perkins, I might bust his head."

"Yeah I know he's a pain in the ass." Moorehouse took out his pipe and tobacco. "Awright, I guess you've done enough today, anyway. I'll get Luke Norton and Jake Vines. I'll have 'em bring those wagons back tonight. They can rest up tomorrow, Dammit, another lost day."

The next morning, Daggett stood next to the supply wagon talking to Moorehouse when he heard a commotion. Two wagons came pulling into the area, led by Norton and Vines. He saw Guthrie, Williams and another fellow that he assumed was Ramsey, But didn't see Perkins. He and Moorehouse rode over to meet them.

"Get Ellie," Williams yelled. "Joe's in the wagon. He's hurt bad."

"What the hell happened to him," Moorehouse asked.

Williams glanced over at Ramsey. "Get Ellie, I'll tell you later."

Moorehouse turned to a man standing nearby. "You! Hurry over and tell Ellie to get here quick, tell her Joe Perkins has been hurt." Then he dismounted. "Which wagon is Joe in?"

Williams climbed down from his horse. He's in the Guthrie wagon. He led them to the wagon, and jerked the canvas cover back. Perkins lay on his back, moaning. Two women knelt next to him.

Moorehouse looked at Perkins and back at Williams. "What the hell happened, Nate? Did Guthrie do this?"

Williams shook his head. "No, Ramsey did it. You know how Joe is. He kept ridin' Guthrie and Ramsey about their fishin' and shootin' their own ox. Guthrie took it, but Ramsey turned on him. He jerked Joe off his horse and started beatin' on him. And while Joe was layin' there on the ground, Ramsey started kickin' him. I swear, Andy, If I hadn't pulled my gun on him I think he'd of killed poor old Joe. Even then he wouldn't stop 'till I fired my pistol in the air."

"Who's the women?" Daggett asked.

"Ramsey's wife and Mrs Guthrie. They've been taken' care of him the best they can. Ain't much they can do, though."

Just then, Ellie showed up. "Someone told me Joe Perkins was injured. What happened?"

Moorehouse said, "He took a pretty good beatin', Ellie." Then he and Daggett helped her up into the wagon. She looked at the women. "Who are you?"

"I'm Mrs. Ramsey, and this here's Mrs. Guthrie. We've been tryin' to make this gentleman as comfortable as we can. I think he's hurt pretty bad."

Ellie looked at the women and back at Perkins "Who did this?"

The two women exchanged glances. Mrs. Ramsey lowered her eyes. "My husband Tom. He's got a terrible temper. This man was riding Tom pretty bad, but he shouldn't of done this to him. I'm so sorry."

Ellie turned to Moorehouse and Daggett. "Help these two down, then get up here and give me a hand getting Joe undressed."

After they got Perkins' pants and shirt off, Ellie said, "All right, give me some room. I'll let you know what's what after I examine him." Moorehouse and Daggett climbed out of the wagon.

Daggett said, "Whatta you say let's have a talk with this Ramsey feller."

"I think that's a good idea. But I'll do the talkin'."

"What ever you say, Andy."

"I mean it, Dave. We've got enough trouble. I don't want any more."

Ramsey was a big red headed man. He and Guthrie were standing together, talking.

"Which one of you is Ramsey?" Moorehouse asked.

Ramsey stepped forward. "Me."

"We've just been lookin' over your handy work. What was you tryin' to do kill the guy?"

"He had it comin'."

Moorehouse glared at him. "Ain't nobody had that comin'."

"Yeah," put in Daggett. "Joe can be a pain in the ass, but he never deserved what you did to him."

Moorehouse whirled around. "Dave!"

"Sorry, Andy, go on."

"Look," Moorehouse said, "We have our own law out here. When need be we form a kind of a court, and decide what to do. Then…"

"Hold on right there." Ramsey shouted. "You ain't tryin' me in no damned kangaroo court. Like I said before, that bastard asked for it. He got just what he deserved."

Moorehouse turned and looked at Daggett then back at Ramsey. "Well, that leaves you with one of two choices. You do it my way or you leave the wagon train."

Ramsey stared at Moorehouse. "You mean you'd kick me

and my family off this train? Leave us out here on our own? That's not very Christian like."

"Neither is kickin' a man half to death," Daggett said.

Moorehouse held up a hand to silence him and said to Ramsey, "Your family's welcome to stay, but you're not." Then he and Daggett turned and walked away.

When they were out of ear shot, Daggett asked, "How's this gonna work, Andy? I mean he can't stay, but his wife and kid can?"

Moorehouse stopped and stared off into the distance. "Dammit, Dave, I don't know. I've never been confronted with this kinda problem before. Let's go check with Ellie, and see how Joe's doin'."

When they arrived at the Guthrie wagon, Ellie was climbing down.

"How's Joe?" Moorehouse asked.

Ellie ran her hands down the sides of her skirt. "He has some broken ribs and a concussion. We're going to have to move him into another wagon, I don't want him left here."

"Is he gonna be all right?" Daggett asked.

"Yes, but he's going to be laid up for quite awhile."

Moorehouse thought a minute. "I'll talk to Bill Lewis, he lost his wife, and is all alone. He'll have room in his wagon. I'm sure he'll take Joe. And he's only three wagons away from yours"

"Good," said Ellie. "That will allow me to keep a close watch on Perkins."

Late that afternoon Ellie came to see Moorehouse. "Andy, what in the world are you thinking?"

"Whatta you talkin' about?"

"Mrs. Ramsey said that you're putting them off the wagon train. You can't do that."

"Now you wait just a minute. I gave that man a choice. He could stand up for what he done to Joe, or leave. I never said nothin' about his family leavin'."

"I swear, Andy Moorehouse, sometimes I think your lamp's gone out. Don't you ever think before you say something?"

"What?"

"What! Think for a minute. You've put her in an impossible situation. You're giving her a choice of leaving her husband out here, or taking her child and going with him. You know she's not going to leave the safety of this wagon train with her child. And what about those people who loaned them their oxen? They're going to want them back. Good Lord, Andy, he don't even have a horse. What is he going to do, walk across the forty mile desert?"

Moorehouse took off his hat, fiddled with the brim and put it back on. "I'd like to know somethin'. This guy nearly kills Joe Perkins, and you're over here jumpin' on me. Takin' his side."

"I'm not taking anyone's side, Andy. I'm just thinking about his wife and child."

Moorehouse glanced at the prairie, golden in the late summer heat. He filled his pipe with tobacco, tamped it down with a thumb, and lit it. "Awright, I'll talk to him again."

"Good," Ellie said, "let's go."

"Wait a minute, Ellie. I said I'd talk to him, and I will."

"Come on, Andy," she said pulling him by the arm. "There's no time like the present."

"Oh awright, but I'll do the talkin'."

She smiled. "Sure, Andy, whatever you say."

As the two of them walked to the Ramsey wagon, Moorehouse motioned at the tree-lined river. "Take a good look, Ellie, it's gonna be two or three long hot dry days before you see something like that again."

Ellie gazed at the river. "I'll try to keep this image in my mind."

When Moorehouse and Ellie arrived at the Ramsey's wagon, Mrs. Ramsey was sitting outside with her daughter. Moorehouse tipped his hat. "Ma'am. Is your husband about?"

"He's sleeping."

"I gotta talk to him."

Mrs. Ramsey nodded and went to the back of the wagon. "Tom, Tom, Mr. Moorehouse is here to see you."

"Dammit, I told you not to wake me. Whatta you want?"

"I said, Mr. Moorehouse is here to see you."

After a few minutes of rumbling around inside, Ramsey climbed out of the back of the wagon, ran his fingers through his hair, squinted and asked, "Whatta you want, Moorehouse?"

"Well, I've gave a lot of thought about our talk this mornin', and decided to let you and your family stay with the wagon train."

Mrs. Ramsey cupped her hands to her cheeks. "Oh, thank you, Mr. Moorehouse."

"Wait just a damned minute," Ramsey yelled. "If you think—"

"No, you wait just a damned minute," Ellie shouted.

Ramsey turned to her in surprise.

Moorehouse whirled around. "Ellie!"

She held up a hand to silence him. "Mr. Ramsey, Andy is trying to do what's best for you and your family. Apparently he's more concerned about your wife and child than you are. Now you be quiet and listen. You have no horse, and no animals to pull your wagon. There's no way you can survive out here on your own. He's going to allow you to stay with the train. That is if you behave yourself between here and Sutter's Fort. Now, you give some thought to your family. Come on, Andy."

As she walked away, Ramsey stared after her in disbelief.

Moorehouse looked at Ramsey, then hurried to catch up with her.

"Wait up, Ellie."

She turned around, reached out and took him by the shoulders. "You did the right thing, Andy."

"The right thing? I didn't do nothin'. I didn't get a chance to. You done all the talkin'. What in the world got into you?"

"Look, Andy, You're a very hubristic man. So I had—"

"Now just you hold on there, Ellie. They ain't no need for you to go callin' me names."

Ellie smiled. "You're a man with a lot of pride, Andy. And this Ramsey fellow is a man who is next to impossible to deal with. So I simply told him what I knew you would have told him yourself only without your pride getting in the way, causing you to forget about his wife and child. You're a strong man, Andy, and I realize that it's hard for you to comprehend that all men aren't like you. Now, I can't stand around talking. I have folks to see."

Ellie walked off, leaving Moorehouse shaking his head.

CHAPTER TWENTY-THREE

At dusk, Daggett and Moorehouse stood drinking coffee and talking. A cool breeze blew out of the northwest. Daggett said, "I hear you're gonna let Ramsey stay with the train."

Moorehouse gave him a suspicious look. "Where'd you hear that?"

"I don't remember who told me. You know how word travels. Anyway, how'd you handle it?"

Moorehouse took a long sip of coffee. "Ramsey was told more or less that he didn't have no choice but to behave himself, what with his wife and kid to think of."

Daggett grinned. "You done the right thing, Andy."

Moorehouse jerked around and glared at Daggett. "Whatta you mean I done the right thing. Whatta you gettin' at?"

Daggett emptied his coffee cup. "Hell, I don't mean nothin'. I just thought th—."

"No, Dammit, I wanna know why you said what you said."

"Let me see, why did I say what I said?" Daggett gazed up at the few stars that had began to appear, then back at Moorehouse and yelled, "What the hells got into you anyway?"

"Okay," Moorehouse yelled back, "forget it. Now let's go over what we're gonna be doin' the next couple days." He took a deep breath. You'll leave tonight and the rest of us will leave tomorrow mornin' before daylight. With you gettin' a head start and makin better time than we will, I'd say you oughta get to them hot springs a good twelve or fourteen hours ahead of the rest of us. Now, Bob Weaver and Wade O'Neil has agreed to go along to give you and Red Eagle a hand dammin' up the back flow of them hot springs so the animals can have some cool water when the wagon train gets there." Moorehouse cupped his hands together, stretched his arms out in front of him and yawned. "You'd better get started. I'll see you sometime tomorrow night. I'm gonna turn in."

Daggett rode over to Ellie's wagon where Red Eagle was waiting. Then the two of them sought out Weaver and O'Neil.

As they rode along in the dark, Daggett said, "I appreciate the two of you comin' along. We can use help dammin' up the springs."

"Glad to do it," O'Neil said, "We're curious to see those hot springs anyway. What are they like?"

Daggett thought a minute and grinned. "Picture what you think hell looks like, and that's pretty much it."

"I hear they spew hot water a hundred feet up in the air," Weaver said.

Daggett laughed. "Someone's been pullin' your leg, Bob, I only saw one that spewed water, and it sure weren't close to no hundred feet."

Red Eagle had been listening closely to the conversation and asked, "What make water hot?"

"I don't know," Daggett said, "it just is."

Red Eagle frowned. "That no make sense. Something make water hot. I ask Miss Ellie, she know."

Daggett glared at Red Eagle. "You think she'll know, huh?"

"Yes. She much wise woman."

"Yeah," O'Neil said, "Red Eagle's right. Something heats that water, and I'd like to know what it is too."

Weaver said, "I once heard it's because there's a volcano down below."

"I hope the damned thing don't blow up while we're there," O'Neil chuckled.

Daggett looked over at Red Eagle. "See what you started." Then he turned to O'Neil and Weaver. "We had a schoolteacher on the trip before last, and he told us what makes these springs hot. I didn't say nothin' because it sounded crazy. But he said that there's some stuff deep in the earth called magnet, magna, or somethin' that's real hot. Then when the rainwater seeps down there, this magna, or whatever it is, heats the water until it turns into steam."

Weaver and O'Neil looked at each and broke out laughing. Weaver said, "That's the dumbest thing I ever heard."

Daggett said, "I know it, I told you that's why I didn't say nothin' before."

The four of them rode all night, stopping only twice to give their horses a rest. The desert night sky was beautiful, so clear it seemed to multiply the stars. But in the early morning light the desert became a ghostly scene, a wasteland. No grass, no trees, no life, not even a bird's trill. Daybreak found them still some ten miles from the springs. Around ten o'clock they spotted faint clouds of steam in the distance. Weaver and O'Neil spurred their horses on, anxious to see the hot springs.

When Daggett and Red Eagle caught up, O'Neil and Weaver were jumping around like two children on Christmas morning.

"Hey," shouted Weaver, "I thought you said one of these springs squirted water in the air."

Daggett climbed off his horse. "One of 'em does." He looked around. "I don't remember which one, but it goes off every once and awhile."

The place was eerie. A warm damp vapor hung in the air and the entire area reeked with a sulfuric smell.

"Christ," Weaver said, "This place smells like rotten eggs."

"It's the sulfur," Daggett said.

"Which one of these springs are we gonna dam up?" O'Neil asked.

"The one we worked on the last time we were through here. It shouldn't be hard to find. It might still have water in it."

They spread out checking all the springs.

"Here it is," O'Neil yelled. "The middle's all washed away, but it's got a little pool of water."

Weaver untied a short handled shovel from his saddle. "Might as well get started," he said. The four of them took turns with the shovel. They had to work fast, trying to get the second shovelfull of dirt in place before the first one washed away.

"Wait a minute," O'Neil said. "Why don't we pick out a spring where the water ain't flowin' so fast? It'd make it a lot easier."

"Can't do that," Daggett said. "Them other springs might be easier, but we'd have a smaller pool of water. There's a lotta livestock, and we wanna make sure there's plenty of water for all of 'em."

"Yeah," Weaver said, "and what if we picked out the one that blows up?"

The short handled shovel was a back breaker, but after two hours they had a dam built up, and a huge pool of water was forming below the spring.

O'Neil put his hand into the pool. "Hey," he said, "it's coolin' off already."

"You got any idea when the wagon train'll show up?" Weaver asked.

Daggett pulled out his pocket watch and looked at it. "I'd say around nine, or ten o'clock tonight. Depends on whether they lose some of their animals or wagons. And if they don't have a run in with the Paiutes."

Weaver frowned. "How come the Paiutes didn't jump us? There's only four of us."

"Four armed men on horseback is one thing, but a slow movin' wagon train with oxen and mules stragglin' along is more to their likin'. They want the oxen and mules."

There was a sudden roar from a nearby spring, and a stream of water shot into the air.

"Good Lord," Weaver said. "Would you look at that. That ain't no hundred feet, but ain't that something?"

When the geyser settled down, Daggett yawned and said, "We oughta get some rest. But one of us better stay awake."

"I stay wake," Red Eagle said.

Daggett took out his watch and walked over to Red Eagle. "Look," he said, holding the watch out. "When these little hands—"

"What hands?" Red Eagle asked, looking at the watch.

Daggett moved closer to him and held out the watch. "See these two little things here?"

Red Eagle studied the watch. "I see."

"Well they're called hands. Now...."

"Wait minute," Red Eagle broke in. "No hands. Arrows."

Daggett frowned at Red Eagle. "They may look like arrows, but they're called hands."

"Why?"

"Dammit, I don't know why, they just are. Now be quiet and listen up. When they get straight up and down," and he moved his finger up and down from the numeral twelve and six, "wake me up. You understand?"

"I understand, Dave Daggett."

"You're sure now?"

"I sure, Dave Daggett."

Red Eagle spent the afternoon keeping a close eye on Daggett's pocket watch, worried that he might not get it right. When the little hand was at six he watched the big hand slowly climb upward. When both were straight up and down he shook Daggett awake and held the watch in front of his face. "Little hand big hand say wake up, Dave Daggett."

Daggett sat up, stretched, looked around and said, "You'd better get some sleep, Red Eagle."

Red Eagle gave him a puzzled look. "I sleep tonight when wagon train get here."

"No, you wont. As soon as the livestock's watered and rested we're gonna push on."

"Wagon train no stay here tonight?"

"That's right, the wagon train no stay here tonight, so you'd better get some sleep while you can."

Red Eagle handed the watch to Daggett and said, "When little hand big hand point up down, you wake me up."

Daggett took the watch. "Yeah, I'll be sure and do that, Red Eagle."

Shortly after sundown, Daggett, Weaver and O'Neil sat talking. Red Eagle was still sleeping.

O'Neil held up his hand. "Quiet. Did you hear that?"

The other two fell silent. There was a squeaky sound in the distance. "That's the wagons," Daggett said. He took out his watch and squinted at it. "Damn, they made good time."

He walked out to meet the train. When Moorehouse recognized Daggett, he spurred his horse on.

Daggett said, "Damn, Andy, you made good time. No Indian trouble?"

"None," said Moorehouse, "and would you believe we only lost two animals"?

"Well, it's about time something good happened."

Moorehouse looked toward the springs "You got water for us?"

"Yeah, there's a good size puddle, and gettin' bigger all the time."

"Well, let's have a look see."

Moorehouse scanned the pool of water then, stuck his hand in it., "Awright, we'll get the animals watered and fed, let 'em rest a couple hours, and then finish this part of the trip." He looked around. "Where's Red Eagle?"

"He's sleepin'. I'd better wake him up." He found Red Eagle curled up sound asleep, and shook him awake. "Rise and shine, Red Eagle, it's time to get up."

Red Eagle sat up, rubbed the sleep from his eyes, and said, "Little hand big hand say time wake up?"

"Yeah, they say time wake up."

Three hours later after the animals had been watered and rested, the wagon train moved out. Daggett and Red Eagle scouted ahead, but not far from the wagons. At ten 0' clock the next morning someone let out a mighty whoopee. The weary travelers gazed upon a beautiful sight, a row of cottonwood trees growing along the Truckee River. After what they had endured the past forty-eight hours, it was indeed a heavenly sight.

Moorehouse gathered his crew together. "Pass the word that we'll spend the rest of the day here. Everybody get watered and rested, and repair any damage to the wagons. We'll move out at first daylight tomorrow."

Early next morning the wagon train was again on the move. Though water and grass was plentiful, it was a hard up grade pull, but nothing like it would be when they started up the mountain trail. The surrounding terrain forced the wagons to have to cross the river many times on boulder strewn fords through icy swift water. Those who earlier had praised the river now cursed it. Everyone was happy when the day's travel ended.

CHAPTER TWENTY-FOUR

Ellie and Red Eagle had just finished their supper, and she was gathering up the plates when Andy Moorehouse showed up. "Ellie, you've gotta come quick. Lon Spencer's wife is bad sick."

She stopped what she was doing and asked, "What's wrong with her?"

"A belly ache. She's in a lotta pain."

Ellie turned to Red Eagle. "Finish cleaning up here. I'll be right back."

She and Moorehouse hurried to the Spencer wagon. Mrs. Spencer was curled up in a fetal position, whimpering. Her husband sat next to her holding her hand. When Ellie entered, He moved out of the way. "She's hurtin' awful bad," he said.

Ellie felt the woman's forehead, then began her examination, pushing on Mrs. Spencer's abdomen, beginning at the navel, then working outward. Each push brought a moan from the woman. Moorehouse felt uncomfortable watching, so he turned and stared out the back of the wagon.

Ellie finished her examination, then turned to Mister Spencer. "How long has she been like this?"

"A couple days."

"Two days? Why in God's name didn't you let me know earlier?"

"I just figured it was a belly ache from somethin' she ate. Is she gonna be awright?"

"She has appendicitis. Heat some water and get me clean towels. I'll be right back." Ellie climbed down from the wagon and went after her medical bag, knowing she would have to operate on the woman, something she prayed that she wouldn't have to do on this journey. Ellie checked the bag to make sure she had everything she would need.

"What matter, Miss Ellie?" Red Eagle asked.

"I can't talk now," she answered and hurried toward the Spencer wagon.

Moorehouse met her half way. Ellie knew by the look on his face what he was going to say.

"She's gone Ellie."

Ellie put the bag down. "If only he had told me when she first complained."

"Don't mention that to him, Ellie."

She glared at him. "Give me a little credit, Andy, I lost my only child to appendicitis. I know how he feels."

Moorehouse took off his hat and started fumbling with the brim. "Sorry, Ellie, I uh, wasn't thinkin'."

"I know, Andy, I shouldn't have hollered at you."

They went back to the wagon. Mr. Spencer sat next to his wife. He looked up when they entered.

"She didn't want to come on this trip, you know. I talked her into it, told her we'd make a new life." He broke down, sobbing.

Ellie leaned over and put her hand on his shoulder. "This could have happened anywhere, Mr. Spencer, you can't blame yourself." Then she turned to Moorehouse and whispered, "Stay with him, I'm going to get some of the women to help me with Mrs. Spencer. When I get back take him to another wagon."

During the night, several men pitched in and dug a grave. One of them fashioned a wooden cross and burned Mrs. Spencer's name on it. The next morning a funeral service was held. When the service ended, folks paid their respects. Then began readying their wagons to move out, except for Spencer. He stayed behind standing at his wife's grave. Ellie spotted him, stopped her wagon, and climbed down. "Come on, Mister Spencer, You have to go now."

He kept staring at the grave, "I can't leave her out here I just can't."

They stood side by side looking at the grave. Ellie gazed at the mountains. "Lon, I know how you feel. I left a son and husband buried back in Maryland. Chances are I'll never see their graves again. It's a hard thing to deal with, but we have to go on with life. We have no choice."

Lon Spencer turned and faced her. "One big difference, Miss. you know where they're buried, you know their graves are cared for, and if ever you went back there, you could visit them. But I know when I leave here I'll never see her grave again. Even If one day I came back, I could never find this place. Then he sat down, put his hand on the mound of dirt and began to cry. "I wish I'd listened to her. All she wanted to do was care for her vegetable garden and her flowers. Oh God, how can I leave her here."

Ellie knelt down next to him, and put an arm around his shoulder. "Please Mister Spencer, you can't stay here."

He stood up. "I'll catch up later."

"Would you like for me to stay with you?"

"No. I want to spend a little time here, alone."

"All right, Lon, we'll be waiting for you."

CHAPTER TWENTY-FIVE

The next morning there was a chill in the air and a light frost. The altitude made the difference.

There was still no sign of Lon Spencer so Ellie talked with Andy Moorehouse about sending someone back to check on him.

"Dammit, Ellie, I can't go sendin' men all over the place ever ti—"

"Now just a minute, Andy," she said, stopping him in mid-sentence. "It's not as if you're sending men out on a wild goose chase, and it's not going to hold up the wagon train. All I'm asking is that you send a couple of men back to check on a grieving man who just lost his wife, and is probably not thinking straight. I can't believe that's asking too much."

Moorehouse took off his hat and slapped it against his leg. "Dammit, Ellie you have a way of makin' a man feel like a lowdown—I don't know what, if you don't get your way. Awright, I'll send someone back to check on him." He jammed his hat back on and stalked off.

Ellie smiled and muttered under her breath, "I knew you would."

Moorehouse located Luke Norton and Jake Vines and explained to them what he wanted. "You'll more then likely meet him on the trail. Without wagons you two oughta make good time. I wouldn't ask you to do this, but you know this is a grievin' man that just lost his wife, and probably ain't thinkin' straight, and I'm worried about him. I'll make it up to you on down the line."

"Okay," said Norton. The two men rode off.

The wagon train moved out. The days travel was a lot like the day before, a steady up grade pull, however they weren't forced to ford the stream as many times, which made a big difference. That evening, Ellie sought out Moorehouse. She asked, "When do you think Norton, Vines and the Spencer wagon will catch up with us?"

"Gosh, Ellie, I don't know. With just one wagon they'll make a lot better time then us, but it'll probably be another day. Maybe two."

The next day's travel was a mess. A team of mules was spooked by the swift water and tried to turn downstream. The wagon was hit broadside by the rushing water and turned over. Another broke an axle. Moorehouse decided to suspend travel for a day to repair the damaged wagon and give the folks whose wagon overturned time to dry out their belongings.

Around one o'clock the following afternoon, Daggett and Moorehouse were standing next to the supply wagon drinking coffee when Luke Norton and Jake Vines rode into camp.

"Where's Spencer?" Moorehouse asked.

"Hell, I don't know," Norton said. "Him and his wagon was gone."

"Yeah," Vines chimed in, "and you know what? There was a gold locket and chain, hangin' on the grave marker."

"Now why in hell did he go and do somethin' like that?" Daggett asked. "You took it didn't you?"

"I was goin' to, but Luke wouldn't let me have it. 'No, no 'he said.' Lon put it there. You leave it alone.'"

Daggett shook his head. "The Indians will take it."

"That's what I told Luke."

"Awright," Moorehouse said. "Forget the locket, what about Spencer? Did you try to catch up to him?"

Norton said, "We rode about five miles back down the trail but didn't see no sign of him. He's probably on his way back to Pennsylvania."

Daggett said, "He'll never make it. The Paiutes'll see to that."

Moorehouse stared off into the distance. "I don't think he cares. Poor bastard." Then as an after thought, he said, "Oh hell, now I've gotta tell Ellie."

Vines shook his index finger at the rest of them. "You know, this is the very reason why I ain't never got married."

Daggett grinned. "Yeah, that and you're so Gawdamned ugly."

Moorehouse spotted Ellie coming his way. He knew she had seen Luke Norton and Jake Vines, and not wanting to talk with her in front of the other men he hurried to meet her.

"Andy, I see Luke and Jake are back. What's going on? Where is Lon Spencer?"

"I'm afraid I got some bad news, Ellie. When they got back where we last saw him, he weren't there."

Ellie frowned. "Well didn't they try to find him?"

Moorehouse took off his hat and started fumbling with the

brim. "Sure they did. In fact they went back down the trail fifteen, maybe twenty miles or more, but never seen hide nor hair of him. I reckon he's on his way back home."

She stared at him. "Andy Moorehouse, you know better then that. Lon Spencer won't last two days out there by himself. The Indians will take his wagon and everything he has."

"Well dang it, Ellie, what was I supposed to do, hog-tie him and put him in a wagon?"

She glared at him. "Maybe that or you could've just shot him." Before Moorehouse could answer, she turned and stalked off.

The wagon train finally left the river and started through Dog Valley, wending its way among the huge pine trees. The pulling was hard with ups and downs, but at least the troublesome Paiutes were left behind. And deer meat was plentiful.

Daggett and Red Eagle rode along some three or four miles ahead of the wagons. The mornings were cold and both were bundled up.

Red Eagle looked over at Daggett. "How long we get to where we go?"

Daggett grinned. "How long we get to where we go? It'll be awhile yet. You getting' in a hurry?"

"We there before tree change color?" Red Eagle asked, pointing at an aspen.

"We'd better be. Why, you worried?"

"No. Miss Ellie worried. She say snow bad."

"Only if we're still in the mountains when it falls. But we won't be."

They rode along in silence for several minutes. Then Red Eagle spoke again, "Miss Ellie much mad at Andy Moorehouse."

Daggett grinned. "Gosh, whatta surprise."

"I hear her say to Andy Moorehouse his fault Spencer man leave wagon."

"She can't blame Andy for Spencer leavin' the wagon train."

"You say her that? I no like when she mad."

"You're damned right I'll say her that."

That evening after supper, Daggett went to see Ellie. She was leaning against the back of the wagon, leafing through a book. When she saw Daggett she put the book down. "Hello Dave, Is there something you need?"

Daggett took off his hat. "Yeah. I hear you're mad at Andy."

She smiled. "And I wonder where you heard that?"

"Ellie, you can't blame Andy for Spencer leavin' the train."

Ellie stared at him for a moment before answering. "I don't blame Andy because Lon Spencer left, but I do blame him for doing nothing to stop him. He did absolutely nothing."

"And you, Ellie. What'd you do?" She didn't answer. "Look, Ellie, I know how you feel. I felt the same way when Dorie and her folks left the train. And I took it out on Andy, too. I was really mad because I didn't get to tell her goodbye. But I blamed him." Daggett took a deep breath and put his hat back on. "I blame him, you blame him. I wonder how many other people blame him for anything that don't go their way? I'm tellin' you, Ellie, Andy's got one helluva job runnin' this wagon train. He can't satisfy everyone. I wouldn't have his job. I couldn't handle it." They stood, silent for some time, then Daggett said, "You know, Ellie, My Mama used to say, 'When life treats you bad, you do three things, cry, build a bridge, and get over it.'"

Ellie smiled. "It sounds like your mama was a very smart woman."

Daggett kicked at a pebble. "She never had a lotta schoolin', but she did a lotta livin'."

Ellie said, "I'm glad we had this talk Dave. I have to go now."

"You got a patient to see?"

"No," Ellie smiled. "I have a bridge to build."

CHAPTER TWENTY-SIX

Daggett and Moorehouse sat on their horses beside a lake, looking at the eastern trail of the Sierra Nevada Mountains. Daggett said, "It's sure pretty ain't it? The pass I mean, with the crags above the trail, and all."

"Not to me," Moorehouse said. "Not when you've gotta get up this side and down the other before it snows. To me it's the last barrier between here and the Sacramento Valley." He turned and looked at Daggett. "Reckon you forgot what a job it was last trip?" Then he paused and said, "Oh, I'm sorry, I keep forgettin', you always ride up ahead of us. You wouldn't know."

Daggett leaned forward and patted his horse's neck, smiled and shook his head.

Moorehouse stood up in his stirrups and looked all around. "Well I'd better get this train movin'. You and Red Eagle don't get too far ahead. Keep in touch. Who knows, we might need your help this time."

"Yeah, Daggett said, "we'll stay within cussin' distance. Course that could be a pretty far distance."

Daggett went by Ellie's wagon and picked up Red Eagle. Not wanting to get too far ahead of the wagons they rode along at a slow pace.

Red Eagle looked over at Daggett. "Miss Ellie no mad at Moorehouse now."

Daggett grinned. "Well, well, she must've built a bridge. I'm glad to hear that."

"She do what?" asked Red Eagle.

"Never mind."

Red Eagle turned in his saddle. "No, I want know what Miss Ellie do."

"And I said never mind. Now forget it."

They rode along quietly, Red Eagle pouting, and mumbling, "I ask Miss Ellie."

Finally he broke the silence. "This not bad hill."

Daggett grinned. "Well, first, this ain't no hill, and second, no, it ain't hard if you're horseback. It's a little different if you're pullin' a loaded down wagon."

Red Eagle said, "We go all way top on trail. I think not bad."

"Yeah, it wouldn't be if the trail went all the way to the top just like it is now, but we've gotta work our way along some forrest ridges and up and down a couple of canyons."

Red Eagle stared straight ahead and murmured, "I think not bad."

Daggett reined his horse to a stop. "You know somethin', Red Eagle? If you say not bad one more time, I'm gonna send your butt back to the wagons for a few days. Then we'll see if you think it not bad."

Daggett and Moorehouse stood next to the supply wagon drinking coffee. Daggett looked back down the line of wagons. "Well, so far so good, huh?"

"Moorehouse emptied his coffee. "Yeah I guess you could say that. We've been lucky. 'Course there's a few that would disagree, like them that had to off load a bunch of their belongin's. Some of the other wagons was able to help out, but not many. That's the folks I feel sorry for. The ones I don't feel sorry for are them that had trouble because they was too damned lazy to take care of their wagons. Like greasin' the axles. I told everyone before we started to take care of stuff like that. He shook his head back and forth. 'Course goin' down the other side seems to always be the problem. Don't look like it'd be that way, but it is."

Daggett slapped at a flying bug with his hat. "I think the wagons and animals take such a beatin' goin' up that they start fallin' apart goin' down."

"Well," Moorehouse said, "I'll tell you one thing, I'll shore be glad when I see old Sutter's Fort."

The trip down the west side was rough down hill going with the danger of broken axles and tongues. Some snubbed ropes around trees, to ease the wagons down, while others tied ropes around and through the wagon spokes of the rear wheels. Even when they made it down the other side, they still had a week or more working their way along forested ridges and across two canyons. But finally in mid-October after five months and two thousand miles travel, the adobe wall of Sutter's Fort came into sight.

After a couple of day's rest for the people as well as the animals, the weary travelers began going their separate ways. There was sadness. With all the hardships they had shared, a bond was formed. They were like veteran soldiers who had been through many campaigns together, parting.

Daggett sat on the ground with his back against the adobe building smoking a new pipe he had just bought. Red Eagle walked up and sat down next to him. "That smoke stunt growth," he said.

Daggett took a big puff and blew it in Red Eagle's face. "And who told you that, Ellie?"

Red Eagle fanned the smoke away with both hands. "No, my friend, Ledbetter tell me."

"Awright, Red Eagle whatta you want? I know you want somethin'"

"I want Gray Cloud knife. You say you get knife. You get knife now?"

Daggett tapped the pipe against the wall, knocking the burnt tobacco out of the bowl and got to his feet. "Joe Perkins has got your knife, C'mon, we'll go get it."

"Not my knife. Gray Cloud knife."

Daggett looked at Red Eagle, but didn't say anything.

They found Perkins trying to resole a pair of boots. When the two of them walked up, he stopped what he was doing and stared at Red Eagle. He turned to Daggett and said "Hello Dave."

"How you doin', Joe? The last time I saw you, you was in pretty bad shape."

"Yeah. And Andy should've throwed that sonofabitch off this train."

"Well, I guess Andy was thinkin' 'bout the guy's wife and kids."

"To hell with his wife and kids." Perkins shouted. "Whatta I care 'bout his wife and kids after what he done to me."

Daggett wished he hadn't brought up the incident. It had put Perkins in a bad mood. Not what he wanted. "Look, Joe, now that this trip's over, Red Eagle wants to go home, but he can't go back without that knife of his you've got. So whatta you say…"

"Why can't he go back without it. What'd he do, steal it?"

"Well—yeah, he did steal it, but he wants to give it back so how about it Joe? Give him the knife."

"Hell no, he stabbed me with that knife. He ain't gettin' it back."

"Dammit, he was scared, you'd just shot him in the leg." Daggett held out his hand. "Now, give me the knife."

"I told you, he ain't gettin' the knife. Now, go on and leave me alone."

"You know, Joe, that ass whoopin' you got didn't learn you nothin'. Now, give me the damned knife."

Perkins pulled the knife out of its scabbard and stared at Daggett and Red Eagle. "If you want this knife you're gonna have to take it."

Daggett took a step forward, reached out and said, "C'mon, Joe, hand it over."

Perkins slapped at Daggett's hand with the knife, cutting him across the palm, just then a large rock hit Perkins squarely in the chest, knocking him down. He rolled over on his side, gasping for air.

Red Eagle ran over, reached down, pulled the scabbard from Perkins' belt and picked up the knife. He Looked down at Perkins, and then at Daggett. "I hurt him bad?"

"Don't you worry 'bout it. You did good." Daggett wrapped a bandana around his hand and said "C'mon, I've gotta find Ellie."

Ellie watched Red Eagle and Daggett approaching. When they walked up she saw the bloodied bandana around Daggett's hand. "Well, Dave, what in the world have you done to yourself now?"

He unwrapped the bandana and held his hand out to her. "I got cut with a knife."

Ellie took his hand and examined the wound. "All right, how did you manage this?"

He told her what happened. Then he grinned. "It might've been worse if Red Eagle wasn't so good at rock throwin'."

Ellie said, "Let's go to the wagon and I'll take care of that hand." She turned to Red Eagle. "You remember Mrs. Phillips, the lady with the sick child?"

Red Eagle nodded. "I know."

Find her and tell her that I'll look in on them after supper. Understand?"

"I understand," he said and left.

Ellie climbed into the wagon, got her medical bag, and climbed back down. "Lay your hand on the tailgate palm up." She soaked a cotton ball with alcohol. "This is going to sting a little, Dave, so grit your teeth and be a big boy." Then she proceeded to clean the wound.

"My God, Ellie," he said through clinched teeth. "Sting a little? I'd like to know what you call a lot."

Ellie ignored him. "I swear," she said, "that Joe Perkins is more trouble than he's worth. I don't know why Andy keeps him on."

"I suspect this'll be his last trip."

Finished cleaning the wound, she said, "This should be sutured, but I'm not going to do it because the stitches will have to be removed and you're going to be off on your own with no medical help. Then with scissors, tape and gauze, she began making what she called butterflies and stretched them across the wound, pulling the sides together. When she finished, she smeared on some salve, then put on a bandage. "Dave, I want you to listen and listen carefully. I'm going to give you a roll of gauze and some tape. Now, this is important. You must keep the cut clean." Then she dug through her bag and handed him a small tin of ointment. "Smear this on the cut every time you change the bandage, which should be every day. Pick a time, either when you go to bed or when you get up. But do it."

"I will. Now I wanna talk to you about Red Eagle."

Ellie started putting everything back in her medical bag. "If it's about talking him out of going to see the ocean, forget it. I've tried. His mind's made up. He's determined to see what he calls the Ocean Lake. I know one thing, I'd love to be there when he first sees it." She smiled. Can you imagine?"

"There's nothin' we can do?"

"No, Dave, his mind's made up." She put the bag in the wagon and closed the tailgate. "Dave, when are you leaving for Oregon?"

"In a couple days."

She walked over to him. "Dave, you've been a good friend." Then on tiptoes she kissed him on the cheek. "Take care of yourself and give my best to Dorie."

Daggett rode up to Moorehouse's wagon. "Andy I wanna talk to you."

"Yeah and I wanna talk to you too. Tell me what the hell happened with you and Perkins?"

Daggett climbed off his horse and slapped the dust from his pant legs with his hat. "All I wanted was for him to give Red

Eagle back that knife he took from him. I swear, Andy, all I done was reach out for the knife and the crazy bastard cut my hand. I'll tell you one thing, it could've been worse if Red Eagle hadn't got him with that rock."

"I believe you. I figured it was something like that."

Daggett shook his head. "I don't know why you keep him on your crew."

"He's gone. I told him this was his last trip, but he was welcome to ride back to Missouri with us."

"How'd he take it?"

Moorehouse laughed. "Not good. He told me to go to hell, that he weren't ridin' anywhere with me. He packed his gear and rode off."

"Good Riddance I say. Now, Andy, I wanna make you a deal. You know Red Eagle is determined to go see the ocean. Now if you give him the horse he's been ridin', you can take it outta my wages. Whatta you say?"

Moorehouse looked off into the distance then back at Daggett. "Just whatta you figure that horse is worth?"

"I don't know, I trust you'll name a fair price."

"You know somethin', I oughta take you up on your offer." He broke out laughing. "Dammit I gave Red Eagle that horse this mornin' along with the saddle. Why in hell didn't you come around here with this deal yesterday?"

"You gave him the horse and the saddle?"

"Hel,l he earned it. You know that."

"I'm still worried about him. He's just a kid. A gullible little shit at that."

"Look, Dave, I've got a few years on you, and there's one thing I've learned about these youngsters; they've got big ideas and all that, but give 'em a couple days off by themselves and they change their tune. More'n likely Red Eagle'll be back here before you know it."

Daggett shook his head. "I hope you're right, Andy."

"Well, if he shows back up here I'll see that he gets home all right."

"Thanks, Andy. I'm still gonna try to talk him out of leavin'" Moorehouse grinned. "Good luck."

Red Eagle was saddling his horse when Daggett approached. "Red Eagle, I wanna talk to you."

Red Eagle stopped what he was doing. "What want, Dave Daggett?"

"I want you to put this silly notion outta your head about goin' to see the ocean."

Red Eagle went back to saddling his horse. "I tell you I got see ocean lake and find sea shells. I take back to Gray Cloud. I give him sea shells and knife. Then he maybe no be mad."

"Look, Red Eagle, Andy said you can ride back with him and the other men as far as your home. Then you can give Gray Cloud his knife back. Dammit that oughta be enough."

Red Eagle swung up on his horse. "I go now, Dave Daggett."

"Wait a minute," Daggett yelled. Where is Ellie? Does she know you're leavin'?

"I no tell her. I no like goodbye"

"Dammit, you gotta tell her. You'll hurt her feelin's if you just ride off without sayin' anything. She likes you."

Red Eagle frowned. "I like too. That why I no like goodbye. You say for me?"

Daggett shook his head. "Awright I say for you. But you listen now. Andy and his bunch are gonna be here for awhile.

So if you change your mind about goin' all the way to the ocean, come on back here."

Red Eagle said, "Now I go," and started to ride off, then stopped and pulled the pistol from his waistband and held it out to Daggett. Daggett reached for it, then stopped. "No, Red Eagle, if you're determined to go, you keep the pistol. But keep it outta sight."

Red Eagle's face lit up. "Thank you Dave Daggett." He looked at Daggett for a minute, and said, "You like brother." Then he spurred his horse.

Daggett watched Red Eagle until he was out of sight and whispered "Take care little brother."

Andy Moorehouse and Ellie stood next to her wagon saying their goodbyes.

"Look, Ellie," he said. "I know we've had our differences, but I want you to know th…"

Ellie reached out and put two fingers across his mouth. "Please, Andy, let's not talk about things that happened on the trip."

Andy took off his hat. "Ellie, I want you to know that of all the women I've met, you're…well, different."

"Is that good or bad?" she said, smiling.

He put his hat back on. "Dammit, Ellie, what I'm tryin' to say is that I'm gonna miss you."

"And I'll miss you too, Andy Moorehouse. You're a good man. I'll always remember you." As she turned away he said "just a minute, Ellie." She stopped. Andy took a piece of paper from his pocket and handed it to her. "This is my address back in Missouri. When you get settled, write to me and let me know where you are. I wanna know you're all right "

Ellie walked over and on tiptoes kissed him on the cheek. "I'll do that, Andy, and thank you for caring."

And that's the way it was: Red Eagle went in search of the ocean lake. Ellie went in search of a place to set up her practice, Daggett went to Oregon in search of Dorie, and Andy Moorehouse and his crew went back to Missouri to do it all over again.

EPILOGUE

Ellie inspected the place she had purchased from Doctor Thomas Bartlett, the town's only doctor. It was located on the north end of Main Street. A small building with only two rooms, but that was all that was needed. A wood cabinet stood in a corner of the treatment room containing the medical records of Doctor Bartlett's patients, which she would have to study carefully. For more than a year Doctor Bartlett had let it be known that he wanted to retire, but he was reluctant to give up his practice and leave the town without a physician, so when Ellie showed up, he gave her a fair sale that included all of his medical equipment. Ellie looked around the place and knew this is where she would live out the remainder of her life. *Now,* she thought, *I have a letter to write.*

* * * * *

Dorie came out of the house with a basket of laundry. On the way to the clothesline she saw a lone horseman approaching.

Wary of strangers, she sat the basket down and shaded her eyes. Suddenly, she lifted her skirt and began running toward the rider.

Daggett reined his horse to a stop, jumped off and ran to meet her. They fell into each other's arms. Dorie laid her head on his chest. "I didn't know if I'd ever see you again," she said, sobbing.

Daggett took her face in his hands. "I told you I'd find you."

* * * * *

Red Eagle stood motionless, looking out at the Pacific Ocean, watching thundering waves crash onto the beach, sending water skimming across the sand right up to his feet. Never in his wildest dreams did he think a body of water could be this big and noisy, even though Ellie had told him so. He was completely in awe of the immense ocean, and the crashing waves. He wondered what caused the water to roll the way it did. He also wondered if his people would believe him when he described it to them.

Red Eagle searched up and down the beach for seashells, discarding the broken ones and keeping those that were intact which wasn't very many. He carefully put them into a small leather pouch and headed back to his horse, which he had tied some distance from the water, fearing the ocean noise might scare the animal. He hung the pouch on the saddle horn and returned to the water's edge where he waited for another wave to roll in. When it receded, he chased it. Then standing with his back to the ocean, he would race the next wave. But the third time the wave won. It knocked him down. He floundered and tumbled like a piece of driftwood. Struggling to his feet, coughing, he wiped the salt water from his eyes and headed back to his horse. Down the beach a ways he spotted a large tree limb that had washed ashore. Red Eagle tore off a piece of bark and put one end in his mouth. It tasted salty. He peeled off two more pieces to take back and show his people.

    Sitting on his horse, Red Eagle took a long last look at the boundless ocean lake. He wanted to remember everything about it: The mist in the air, the sand, the rolling waves, and the majestic sea gulls soaring gracefully along the seashore. He looked down at the bag containing the seashells and the strips of salty bark, then reaching down he fingered Gray Wolf's knife and said aloud, "Now I go home."